The Boy Scout's Mountain Camp Vol.I

John Henry Goldfrap

Edition : Culturea (Hérault, 34)
Contact : infos@culturea.fr
Print in Germany by Books on Demand
Design and layout : Derek Murphy
Layout : Reedsy (https://reedsy.com/)
ISBN : 9791041950911
Légal deposit : September 2023

The Boy Scouts' Mountain Camp Vol.I

CHAPTER I.

A TYPICAL BOY SCOUT.

"Hullo, Rob; what's up?"

Merritt Crawford stopped on his way past the Hampton postoffice, and hailed Rob Blake, the leader of the Eagle Patrol, of which Merritt was corporal. Both lads wore the natty scout uniform.

"Not a thing is up or down, either," rejoined Rob, with a laugh; "it looks as if things had stopped happening in Hampton ever since that schooner was blown up."

"And Jack Curtiss's hopes of a fortune with it," added Merritt. "Well, I'm off home. Going that way?"

"Yes, I'll be with you in a Hullo, what's happening?"

From farther up the street, at one end of which lay the glistening sheet of water known as Hampton Inlet, there came excited shouts. Then, suddenly, into the field of vision there swept, with astonishing rapidity, a startling sight.

A large automobile was coming toward them at a rapid rate. On the driver's seat was a whitefaced young girl, a cloud of fair hair streaming out about her frightened countenance. She was gripping the steering wheel, and seemed to be striving desperately to check the onrush of the machine. But her efforts were vain. The auto, instead of decreasing its rate of progress, appeared every minute to be gaining in speed.

It bumped and swayed wildly. A cloud of yellow dust arose about it. Behind the runaway machine could be perceived a crowd of townsfolk shouting incoherently.

"Oh, stop it! I shall be killed! Stop it, please do!"

The young girl was shrilly screaming in alarm, as the machine approached the two boys. So rapidly had events progressed since they first sighted it, that not a word had been exchanged between them. All at once, Merritt noticed that he was alone. Rob had darted to the roadway. As the auto dashed by, Merritt saw the young leader of the Hampton Boy Scouts give a sudden flying leap upon the runningboard. He shot up from the road as if a steel spring had projected him.

For one instant he hung between life and deathor, at least, serious injury. The speed with which the auto was going caused the lad's legs to fly out from it, as one of his hands caught the side door of the tonneau. But in a jiffy Rob's athletic training triumphed. By a supreme effort he managed to steady himself and secure a grip with his other hand. Then he rapidly made his way forward along the runningboard.

But this move proved almost disastrous. The already panicstricken girl took her attention from the steeringwheel for an instant. In that molecule of time, the auto, like a perverse live thing, got beyond her control. It leaped wildly toward the sidewalk outside the Hampton candy store. A crowd of young folksit was Saturday afternoonhad been indulging in ice cream and other dainties, when the shouts occasioned by the runaway machine had alarmed them.

Instantly soda and candy counters were neglected, and a rush for the sidewalk ensued. But, as they poured out to see what was the matter, they were faced by deadly peril.

The auto, like a juggernaut, was careening straight at them. Its exhausts roared like the nostrils of an excited beast.

Young girls screamed, and boys tried to drag them out of harm's way. But had it not been for the fact that at that instant Rob gained the wheel, there might have been some serious accidents.

The lad fairly wrenched it out of the hands of the girl driver, who was half fainting at the imminence of the peril. A quick, savage twist, and the car spun round and was on a straight course again. That danger, at least, was over. But another, and a deadlier, threatened.

Right ahead lay the spot where the road terminated in a long wharf, at which occasional steamers landed. Every second brought them closer to it. If Rob could not stop the machine before it reached the end of the wharf, it was bound to plunge over and into the sea. All this flashed through the boy's mind as he strove to find some means of stopping the car. But the auto was of a type unfamiliar to him. One experiment in checking its motion resulted instead in a still more furious burst of speed.

Like objects seen in a nightmare, the stores, the white faces of the alarmed townsfolk, and the other familiar objects of the village street, streaked by in a gray blur.

"I must stop it! I must!" breathed Rob.

But how? Where had the manufacturer of the car concealed his emergency brake? The lever controlling it seemed to be mysteriously out of sight. Suddenly the motion of the car changed. It no longer bumped. It ran terribly smoothly and swiftly.

From the street it had passed out upon the even surface of the planked wharf. Only a few seconds now in which to gain control of it!

"The emergency brake!" shouted Rob aloud in his extremity.

"Your foot! It works with your foot, I think!"

The voice, faint as a whisper over a longdistance telephone, came to the ears of the striving boy. It belonged to the girl beside him. Glancing down, Rob now saw what he would have observed at first, if he had had time to look about hima metal pedal projected through the floor of the car. With an inward prayer, he jammed his foot down upon it. Would it work?

The end of the pier was terribly close now. The water gleamed blue and intense. It seemed awaiting the fatal plunge overboard.

But that plunge was not taken. There was a grinding sound, like a harsh purr, the speed of the car decreased, and, finally, it came to a stopjust in time.

From the landward end of the pier a crowd came running. In front were two or three khakiuniformed members of the Eagle Patrol. Behind them several of the Hawks were mingled with the crowd.

Beyond all the confusion, Rob, as he turned his head, could see another automobile coming. It had two passengers in it. As the crowd surged about the boy and the girl, who had not yet alighted, and poured out questions in a rapid fusillade, the second car came "honking" up.

A murmur of "Mr. Blake" ran through the throng, as a tall, ruddyfaced man descended, followed by a militarylooking gentleman, whose face was strongly agitated. Mr. Blake was Rob's father, and, as readers of other volumes of this series know, the banker and scout patron of the little community. It was his car in which he had just driven up with his companion.

The latter hesitated not a moment, but in a few long strides gained the side of the car which Rob's efforts had stopped just in time.

"Bravely done, my lad; bravely done," he cried, and then, to the girl, "good heavens, Alice, what an experience! Child, you might have been killed if it had not been for this lad's pluck! Mr. Blake," as the banker came up, "I congratulate you on your son."

"And I," rejoined the banker gravely, "feel that I am not egotistical in accepting that congratulation. Rob, this is my friend, Major Roger Dangerfield, from up the State."

"And this," said the major, returning Rob's salutation and turning to the girl who was clinging to him, "is my daughter, Alice, whose first experience with the operation of an automobile nearly came to a disastrous ending."

Rob Blake, whose heroic action has just been described, wasas readers of The Boy Scout Series are awarethe leader of the Eagle Patrol, an organization of patriotic, cleanlived lads, attracted by the high ideals of the Boy Scout movement.

The patrol, while of comparatively recent organization, had been through some stirring adventures. In The Boy Scouts of The Eagle Patrol, for instance, we read how Rob and his followers defeated the machinations of certain jealous and unworthy enemies. They repaid evil with good, as is the scout way, but several despicable tricks, and worse, were played on them. In this book was related how Joe Digby in the camp of the Eagles, was kidnaped and imprisoned on a barren island, and how smoke signaling and quick wit saved his life. The boys solved a mystery and had several exciting trials of skill, including an aeroplane contest, which was almost spoiled by the trickery of their enemy, Jack Curtiss.

In the second volume, The Boy Scouts on the Range, we followed our young friends to the Far West. Here they distinguished themselves, and formed a mounted patrol, known as The Ranger Patrol. The pony riders had some exciting incidents befall them. These included capture by hostile Indians and a queer adventure in the haunted caves, in which Tubby almost lost his life.

In this volume, Jack Curtiss and his gang were again encountered, but although their trickery prevailed for a time, in the end they were routed. A noteworthy feature of this book was the story of the career and end of Silver Tip, a giant grizzly bear of sinister reputation in that part of the country.

The Boy Scouts and the Army Airship, brought the lads into a new and vital field of endeavor. They met an army officer, who was conducting secret tests of an aeroplane, and were enabled to aid him in many ways. In all the thrilling situations with which this book abounds, the boys are found always living up to the scout motto of "Be prepared."

How they checkmated the efforts of Stonington Hunt, an unscrupulous financier, to rob a poor boy of the fruits of his inventive geniusa work in which he was aided by his unworthy son, Freeman Huntmust be read to be appreciated. In doing this work, however, they earned Hunt's undying hatred, and, although they thought they were through with him when he slunk disgraced out of Hampton, they had not seen the last of him.

As the present story progresses, we shall learn how Stonington Hunt and his son tried to avenge themselves for their fancied wrongs at the hands of the Boy Scouts.

CHAPTER II.

TWO MYSTERIOUS MEN.

"Tell us all about it, Rob!"

The Eagles and the Hawks pressed close about Rob, as, after the two machines had driven off, the scouts stood surrounded by curious townsfolk on the wharf.

"Not much to tell," rejoined Rob, with a laugh. "Major Dangerfield is, it appears, an old friend of my father. He comes from Essex County, or rather, he has a summer place up there. On an automobile trip from Albany, to take his daughter to visit some friends down on Peconic Bay, he decided to stop over at Hampton and see the governor.

"He entered the bank to give dad a surprise, leaving his daughter outside for a few minutes, in the machine. She became interested in its mechanism and pulled a lever, andthe machine darted off. Andand that's all," he concluded modestly.

"Except that the leader of the Eagles covered himself with laurels," struck in Bobor TubbyHopkins, another member of the Eagles.

"Better than being covered with fat," parried Rob, who didn't relish this open praise.

"Three cheers for Rob Blake!" yelled Fylan Fobbs, a town character.

"Hip! hip! hooray!"

The cheers rang out with vim, the voices of the young scouts sounding shrill and clear among them, giving the patrol call:

"Kreeeeeee!"

Rob, coloring and looking embarrassed, made his way off while the enthusiasm was at its height. With him went Merritt Crawford, Tubby Hopkins and tall, lanky Hiram Nelson, the New England lad, who had already gained quite a reputation as a wireless operator and mechanical genius of the allround variety.

"Reckon that was a right smart piece of work," drawled Hiram in his nasal accents, as the four of them trudged along.

“Alice, where art thou?” hummed Tubby teasingly, with a sharp glance at Rob. “Say, what a romance for the newspapers: Gallant Boy Scout rescues beeyootiful girl at risk of his life, and”

He got no further. The tormented Rob grabbed the rotund youth and twisted his arm till Tubby yelled for mercy. With a goodnatured laugh, Rob released him.

“Better sue him for damages, if he’s broke your arm,” grinned the practicalminded Hiram, in consolatory tones.

“No, thanks; I’ve got damages enough, as the fellow said who’d been busted up in a railroad accident and was asked if he intended to sue,” laughingly rejoined Tubby; “but”and he dodged to a safe distance“that was a mighty pretty girl.”

As he spoke, they were passing by the railroad station. A train had just pulled out of it, depositing two passengers on the platform. But none of the boys noticed them at the moment. Instead, their attention was attracted by the strange action of Merritt, who suddenly darted to the center of the roadway.

The next instant his action was explained, as he bent and seized a big leather wallet that lay there. Or, rather, he was just about to seize it, when one of the two men who had alighted from the train also dashed from the small depot, in front of which they had been standing.

He was a broadshouldered, roughlooking fellow, with a coarse beard and hulking shoulders. His clothes were rather poor.

“What you got there, boy?” he demanded, as the other Boy Scouts and his own companion came up.

“WHAT YOU GOT THERE, BOY?” HE DEMANDED.

“A wallet,” said Merritt, examining his find; “it’s marked ‘R. D.U. S. A.’”

A strange light came into the roughlooking man’s eyes. His comrade, too, appeared agitated, and gripped the bearded fellow’s arm, whispering something to him.

“Let’s have a look at that wallet, young chap,” quoth the bigger of the two strangers, almost simultaneously.

“I don’t know that I will,” rejoined Merritt; “it’s lost property, and may contain valuables. I had better turn it over to the proper authorities.”

But the rough stranger, without ceremony, made a snatch for it. Merritt, however, was too quick for him, and the fellow missed his grasp. He growled something, and then, apparently thinking the better of his illtemper, said in a comparatively mild voice:

“Guess that’s my wallet, boy. I must have dropped it coming across the street. My name’s Roger Dangerfield, Major Roger Dangerfield, of the United States Army, retired.”

“Then there must be two of them,” exclaimed Rob sharply.

“How’s that? What are you interfering for?” growled the roughlooking man, while his companiona much younger individual than himself, though quite as illfavorededged menacingly up.

“Because,” said Rob quietly, “I had the pleasure of talking to Major Dangerfield a few minutes ago. Moreover, there’s no doubt in my mind that the wallet is his. He probably dropped it on the way up the street.”

The bigger and elder of the two strangers looked nonplussed for an instant, but he speedily recovered himself. Making a snatch for the wallet, which Merritt for an instant had allowed to show from behind his back, he upset the lad by the sheer weight of his attack. Flat on his back fell Merritt, the bearded man toppling over on top of him.

But, as they fell, the Boy Scout’s assailant seized the wallet from him and tossed it hastily to his companion, as one might pass a football. This action was unnoticed by the Boy Scouts, and the younger man of the two strangers darted off instantly, with the pocketbook in his possession.

In the meantime, Merritt, by a wrestling trick, had glided from under the bearded fellow, and, despite his struggles, the man found himself held in the firm grip of four determined pairs of young arms. He was remarkably strong, however, and the situation speedily assumed the likeness of an uneven contest, when another detachment of the

Eagles, headed by little Andy Bowles, the bugler of the Patrol, came up the street on their way from the exciting scene on the wharf.

Aided by these reënforcements, the man was compelled, despite his strength, to give in. All about him surged his excited young captors. At this moment an individual came hurrying up. He wore a semiofficial sort of dress, adorned with a tin badge as big and shiny as a new tin pieplate. It was Si Ketchum, the village constable.

“Hoppin’ watermillions!” he gasped, “what’s all this here?”

It took only a few words to tell him. Si assumed his most terrific official look, which consisted of partially closing his little reddish eyes and screwing up his mouth till his gray goatee pointed outward horizontally.

“Ef so be as you’ve got that thar contraption uv a wallet, in ther name uv ther law I commands yer to surrender said property,” he ordered ponderously.

The bearded man, still panting from his struggle, rejoined with a grin.

“Surely you’re not going to believe a pack of irresponsible boys, constable. I know nothing about the wallet, except that I saw that lad there pick it up.”

“Umhah,” said Si, wagging his head sagely, “go on.”

“Naturally, I was anxious to see what it was. I demanded to have a look at it, thinking it might be some of my property that I had dropped. What was my astonishment, when this young ruffian attacked me. In selfdefense, I resisted, and then they all set on me.”

“That story is a fabrication from start to finish,” cried Merritt, while the others shouted their angry confirmation of his denial. “Let me”

For the second time he was about to relate the true circumstances. But Si interrupted him.

“Only one way ter settle this,” he said.

“Any way you like, officer,” said the bearded man suavely, “anything that you say, I’ll agree to.”

“Air yer willin’ ter be searched?”

“Certainly. But not here in the public street.”

“All right, then; at the calaboose, ef that’ll suit yer better.”

“It will. Let’s proceed there,” said the man, with a sidelong look at the boys, who began to wonder at his assurance.

Followed by a small crowd, Si and his prisoner led the way to the “calaboose,” a small, redbrick structure on a side street not far from the station. The boys waited eagerly outside, while within the walls of Si’s fortress the search went on. Before long, the constable emerged with an angry face, and very red. The stranger, cool and smiling, was beside him.

“What kind uv an April fool joke is this?” demanded Si loudly, while the boys, and the townspeople, who had been attracted by curiosity, looked at him in astonishment.

“You boys ain’t tole me the truth,” he went on, waxing more furious.

“Youyou haven’t found the wallet?” demanded Merritt. “Why, I distinctly felt him snatch it from my hand.”

“Wall, it ain’t on him.”

“The other man!” cried Rob, suddenly recalling the bearded man’s companion, and perceiving, likewise, for the first time since Merritt’s adventure, that the fellow had vanished.

“He’s gone!” cried half a dozen voices.

In the same instant, they became aware that the bearded man had also vanished in the excitement. Almost simultaneously, Major Dangerfield put in an unexpected appearance. He was out of breath, as if from running.

“Is this the police station?” he demanded of Si, and, receiving a nod from that stupefied official, he hastened on:

"I wish to report the loss of a pocketbook. I must have dropped it on Main Street. Has it been found?"

"It wuz found all right," grunted Si, "butit's bin lost agin."

"Corporal Crawford here, found it, sir," struck in Rob, seeing the major's evident agitation at Si's not overlucid explanation, "but while he still had it in his hand, a mana roughlooking customerdemanded to see it. As soon as Merritt told him of the initials on it, he"

"Tried to seize it," exclaimed the major excitedly.

"Why, yes," rejoined Rob, wondering inwardly how the major guessed so accurately what had occurred, "there was a scuffle, and in it the man who had attacked Merritt must, in some way, have found a chance to pass the pocketbook to his companion."

"Was the man who first inquired about the book a big, bearded man, with sunburned face and rather shabby clothes?" inquired the major.

Rob's astonishment increased. Evidently this was no ordinary case of ruffianism. It would seem now that the men were known to the major, and had some strong object in taking the book.

The boy nodded in reply to the major's question.

"Do you mind stepping aside with me a few minutes, my lad? I'd like to ask you some questions," continued the retired officer.

He and Rob conversed privately for some moments. Then the major strode off, after authorizing Si to offer a reward of five hundred dollars for the return of the wallet.

"He asked me to thank all you fellows for the aid you gave in trying to hold the man," said Rob when he rejoined his comrades, "he added that it would not be forgotten."

Nor was it, for it may be said here, that a few days later a fine launch, named Eagle, was delivered at Hampton harbor with a card from the major, begging the Eagle Patrol to accept it as their official craft. But we are anticipating a little.

As Rob walked away with Merritt, Tubby and Hiram, the lanky youth spoke up:

“It beats creation what there could have been in that wallet to upset him so,” he commented; “he doesn’t look like a man who’s easily excited, either.”

“Well, whatever it was,” rejoined Rob, “we are likely to learn this evening. I rather think the major has some work on hand for us.”

“Hooray! some action at last,” cried Merritt enthusiastically.

“Haven’t had enough today, eh?” inquired Tubby sarcastically. “I should think that seeing a runaway auto stopped, being knocked down and plunged into a mystery, would”

“Never mind him, Merritt; the heat’s sent the fat to his head,” laughed Rob.

“I was going to say,” he continued, “that Major Dangerfield has invited us to the house this evening to hear something interesting.”

“All four of us?”

“Yes. I rather think then we shall learn some more about that wallet.”

Soon after, the boys, following some talk concerning patrol matters, separated. Each went to his home to await, with what patience he might, the coming of evening, when it appeared likely that some light would be shed on what, to them, seemed an interesting puzzle. Rob, on his return home, found that the major had motored on to his friend’s with his daughter, but he had promised to return in time to keep his appointment.

CHAPTER III.

THE MAJOR EXPLAINS.

"Well," began the major, "I suppose you are all naturally curious concerning that wallet of mine."

The four lads nodded attentively.

"I must admit we are," volunteered Rob.

They were gathered in the library of Mr. Blake's home. The banker was seated in his own pet chair, while the major stood with his back to a bookcase, a group of eagereyed Boy Scouts surrounding him.

"In the first place," continued the major, "I think you would better all sit down. The story is a somewhat lengthy one."

The boys obeyed, and the major began:

"I shall have to take you back more than a century," he said, "to the days when the first settlers located adjacent to the south banks of Lake Champlain. Among the colonists were my ancestors, Chisholm Dangerfield and his family. Chisholm Dangerfield was the eldest son of the Dangerfield family, of Chester, England. He had been left an ample fortune, but having squandered it, decided, like many others in a similar case, to emigrate to the new country.

"On arrival here, he and his family went up the river to Albany, and there, hearing of new settlements along the lake, decided to take up land there. They went most of the way by water, being much harassed by Indians on the journey. But without any serious mishaps, they finally arrived at their destination, and, in course of time, established a flourishing farm. But Chisholm Dangerfield had a younger brother, a harumscarum sort of youth, to whom, nevertheless, he was much attached. When quite young, this lad had run away to sea, and little had been heard of him since that time.

"But while his family had remained in ignorance of his whereabouts, he had joined a band of West Indian pirates, and in course of time amassed a considerable fortune. Then a desire to reform came over him, and he sought his English relatives. They would have nothing to do with him, despite his wealth, and in a fit of rage he left England to seek his brotherthe only being who ever really cared for him. In due time he arrived at the farm with quite a retinue of friendly Indians and carriers.

"He was warmly welcomed. Possibly his money and wealth had something to do with it. I don't know anything about that, however. At any rate, for some years, he lived there, till one day he fell ill. His constitution was undermined by the reckless, wild life he had led, and he died not long after. He left all his gold and jewels to his brother.

"Indians were many and hostile in those days, so in order to be secure in case of an attack, the elder brother had no sooner buried his kin with due reverence, and received his legacy, than he decided to secrete the entire amount of the old pirate's treasure in a cave in a remote part of the Adirondacks."

"Gee!" exclaimed Tubby, who was hugging his knees, while his eyes showed round as saucers in his fat cheeks.

"Did the Indians get it?" asked Hiram.

"Wait a minute, and you shall hear," continued the major. "Well, as I said, the treasure was buried in a cave so securely hidden that nobody would be able to find it again, except by a miracle, or by aid of the chart of the spot, which Chisholm Dangerfield carefully made. A few nights after that, a tribe went on the warpath, landed in canoes near to the Dangerfield farm, and massacred every soul on the place but onea young boy named Roger Dangerfield, who escaped.

"This Roger Dangerfield was my greatgreatgrandfather. With him, when he fled from the burning ruins, he took a paper his father had thrust into his hands just before the Indian attack came. All this he wrote in his diary, which did not come into my hands till recently. Well, Roger Dangerfield, left to his own resources, proved so able a youth that he was, before very long, a prosperous merchant in Albany. But in the meantime he made several expeditions to the mountains to try to find the hidden wealth.

"I should have told you that the paper was in cipher, and a very elaborate one, so that it had never been completely worked out. This, no doubt, accounts for Roger Dangerfield's failure.

"Well, in course of time, the cipher became a family relic along with Roger Dangerfield's diary. His descendants moved to Virginia, where I was born. I recollect, as a youngster, being enthralled by the story of the old piratical Dangerfield's hidden gold, and resolving that when I grew up I would find it. We had, in our employ at that time, a butler named Jarley. I was an only child, and he was my confidant. I naturally told him about the cipher and what its unraveling would mean.

"This happened when I was about eighteen and home on a vacation. Jarley seemed much interested, but after both he and I had puzzled in vain over the cipher, we gave it up. When I came home on my next vacation, I learned that Jarley had left. His mother and father had died, he declared, and he was required at his home in Maine. Well, I thought no more of the matter, and forming new acquaintances in our neighborhood, which was rapidly settling, I soon forgot Jarley. But one day a notion seized me to look at the cipher and the diary again.

"But when I came to look for them, they had gone. Nor did any search result in my finding them. It at once flashed across my mind that Jarley might have taken them. So fixed an idea did this become, that I visited the place in Maine to which he said he had gone, only to find that he had removed soon after his return from Virginia. However, pursuing the trail, I found that heor a man resembling himhad visited the spot on the lake where the oldtime house had stood, and had made a mysterious expedition into the mountains. The spot was at that time known as Dangerfield, and was quite a flourishing little town, with a pulp mill and a few other local industries. In that quiet community they recollected the mysterious visitor well.

"However, as I learned, Jarley had left the town without paying his guides or the man from whom he had hired the horses, I concluded that the expedition had not been successful. Then I advertised for the man, but without success. Then I was appointed to West Point, and for a long time I thought no more of the matter. In fact, for years it lay dormant in my mind, with occasional flashes of memory; then I would advertise for Jarley or his heirs, but without success.

"The last time I advertised was about a year ago. After six months' silence I received a letter, asking me to call at an address near the Erie Basin in Brooklyn, if I was interested in the longlost Jarley. All my enthusiasm once more at fever heat, I set out for the place. The address at which I was to call I found to be a squalid sailors' boardinghouse. On inquiring there for James Jarley, the name signed to the letter, I was conducted into a dirty room, where lay a roughlooking sailor, evidently just recovering from the effects of a debauch.

“So dulled was his mind, that it was some time before I could explain my errand, but finally he understood. He frankly told me he was out for money, and wanted to know how much I would give him for some papers he had which his fatherour old butler, it transpiredhad left him. His father, he said, had told him that if ever he wanted to make money with them he was to seek out a Major Dangerfield, who would be likely to pay him well for them.

“But it appeared that his father had also told him that he stood a chance of arrest if he did so, and that it might be a dangerous step. However, he told me that he had at length decided to take that chance, and on a return from a long voyage, during which he had encountered my advertisement in an old newspaper in a foreign port, he had made up his mind to find me on his return.

“His father, it appeared, had always kept track of me, but fear and shame had kept him from trying to arrange a meeting. The son, I gathered, both from his conversation and the situation in which I found him, had always been a ne’erdowell. Well, the matter ended with my paying him a sum of money for the papers, which as I suspected, proved to be the yellowpaged old diary and the wellthumbed, tattered cipher. Then I had him removed to a hospital, where a few days later he died in an attack of delirium.”

CHAPTER IV.

THE NARRATIVE CONTINUED.

"But it appeared that even while on his deathbed the man had been playing a dishonest game. Before he had made his bargain with me, he had revealed the secret and tried to sell it to a certain moneylender at a seaport in Maine. This man had refused to have anything to do with what he thought was a chimerical scheme, but later confided the whole thing to a friend of his by name Stonington Hunta former Wall Street man, who had been compelled to quit in disgrace the scene of his financial operations."

"Stonington Hunt!" gasped Rob, leaning forward in his chair, while the others looked equally amazed.

"Yes, that was the name. Why, do you know him?"

"Know him, Major!" echoed Mr. Blake. "He was concerned in some rascally operations in this village not so long ago. That he left here under a cloud, was mainly due to activities of the Boy Scouts, whose enemy he was. We heard he had gone to Maine. Is he engaged in new rascality?"

"You shall hear," pursued the major. "Well, as I said, this seaport moneylender told Stonington Hunt of the chart and cipher and the old diary recording the burial of the treasure. Hunt, it would seem, placed more importance on the information than had the moneylender, for he agreed, provided the latter would help to finance an expedition, to try to solve the cipher, or else have some expert translate it. He set out at once for Brooklyn, arriving there, as I subsequently learned, just after I had departed with the diary and the papers which young Jarley had carried in his seachest for some years.

"He lost no time in tracing me, and offered me a large sum for the papers. But my interest had been aroused. For the sake of the adventure of the thing, and also to clear up the mystery, I had resolved to go treasure hunting myself. With this object in view, I rented a bungalow on a lake not far from the range in which I suspected the treasure cave lay, and devoted days and nights trying to solve the cipher. At this time a college professor, an old chum of mine, wrote me that his health was broken down, and that he needed a rest. I invited him to come and visit me in Essex County, at the same time suggesting that I had a hard nut for him to crack. Professor Jeremiah Jorum arrived soon after, and his health picked up amazingly in the mountain air. One day he asked about 'the hard nut.' I produced the cipher, and told him something of its history.

Perhaps I should have told you that Professor Jorum has devoted a good deal of his life to what is known as cryptologyor the solving of seemingly unsolvable puzzles. He had translated Egyptian cryptograms and inscriptions left by vanished tribes on ruins in Yucatan and Old Mexico.

“He worked for several days on the cipher, and one day came to me with a radiant face. He told me he had solved it. No wonder I had failed. It was a simple enough cipherone of the least complex, in factbut the language used had been Latin, in which my ancestor, as a wellbred Englishman of that day, was proficient. As he was telling me this, I noticed a man I had hired some days before, hanging about the open windows. I ordered him away, and he went at once. But I had grave suspicions that he had overheard a good deal more than I should have wished him to. However, there was no help for it. I dismissed the matter from my mind, and wethe professor and Ispent the rest of the day discussing the cipher and the best means for recovering the treasure. We agreed it would be dangerous to take men we could not absolutely trust, and yet, we should require several people to organize a proper expedition.

“But, as it so happened, all our plans had to be changed that night. I was awakened soon after midnight by a noise in my room. In the dim light I saw a figure that I recognized as our gardener, moving about. The lamp beside my bed had, for some reason, not gone out when I turned it down on retiring, and I soon had the room in a blaze of light. The intruder sprang toward me, a big club in his hand. I dodged the blow and grappled with him. In the struggle his beard fell off, and I recognized, to my amazement, that our ‘gardener’ was Stonington Hunt himself.

“The shock of this surprise had hardly been borne in upon me when the fellow, who possessed considerable strength, forced me back against the table. In the scuffle the lamp was upset. In a flash the place was in a blaze. Hunt was out of the room in two bounds. He seized the key, as he went, and locked the door on the outside, thus leaving me to burn to death, or chance injury by a leap from the window, which overhung a cliff above the lake. I had just time to throw on a few clothes and grab the papers, which I had luckily placed under my pillow, before the flames drove me out. The wood of the door was flimsy, and without bothering to try to force the lock, I smashed out a panel. Crawling through, I aroused my friend Jorum and my old negro servant, Jumbo.

“We saved nothing but the precious papers, but as the bungalow was roughly furnished, I did not much care. We made our way to a distant house and stayed there the night. The next day we took a wagon to the shore of the lake and went by boat to Whitehall. There we embarked on a train for Albany, where my daughter was at the home of friends. I, too, have a residence there, but, having received an invitation from friends to visit them on Long Island, I decided to give my little girl a motor trip.

"But while in Albany I perceived I was being followed, and by the two men whom you have described to me as taking part in the filching of the wallet. I thought I had thrown them off, however, but your adventure today proves that I have not been as successful as I hoped. The most unfortunate part of it is that the cipher was in that wallet."

"And it's gone," groaned Tubby dolorously.

"I'm not so sure of that. I am hopeful that we may recover it," said the retired officer. "I have wired my friend Jorum, who, with Jumbo, is now in New York, and I am in hopes that he can recollect something of his translation of the cipher. If notwell, there's no use crossing bridges till we come to them."

"If you do recover it?" asked Rob.

"If I do, I am going to ask your parents to let me borrow a patrol of Boy Scouts to aid in the treasure hunt," smiled the major.

"My dear Major," cried Mr. Blake, holding up his hands, "Mrs. Blake would never consent to"

"But there would be such a lot of fun, dad," urged Rob. "Think of a camp in the mountains. We'd have to camp, wouldn't we, Major?"

"Certainly. It would be a fine opportunity for you to perfect yourselves in"

"Woodcraft," said Tubby.

"Signaling," put in Merritt.

"I've got a field wireless apparatus I'd like to try out," put in Hiram, his voice aquiver with eagerness.

"Well, the first thing to be done is to recover that cipher," said the major; "at present all we know of it is that it is in the hands of two rascals."

"In the employ of another rascal, Stonington Hunt," put in Rob.

"Well, we can do nothing more tonight," said the major.

"No. We were so interested in your story that I think none of us noticed how the time flew by," said Mr. Blake, and Mrs. Blake, entering just then, announced that there was supper ready for the party in the diningroom. Tubby's eyes glittered at this news.

Soon after the sandwiches, cakes and lemonade had been disposed of, the Boy Scouts set out for home, agreeing to meet the major next morning after breakfast.

They had not gone many steps from the house when Tubby stopped as suddenly as if he had been shot.

"Gingersnaps!" he exclaimed. "I've just thought of something."

"Goodness! Must hurt," jeered Merritt unsympathetically.

"Nothat is, yesno, I mean," sputtered the fat boy. "Say, fellows, I heard this afternoon that Sam Phelps from Aquebogue told a fellow in the village that he had seen Freeman Hunt over there this morning."

"You doubledyed chump," exclaimed Rob, who was walking a way with them, "and you never said anything about it. If Freeman was there, I'll bet his father was, too, and that's where those two men have gone."

"Gee whiz, if they have they must be there yet, then!" exclaimed Merritt, excitedly, "unless they left by automobile."

"How's that?" demanded Rob.

"It's this way. There was no train after those chaps took the wallet, till almost eight o'clock. They must have hidden in the woods and caught it some place below, unless Si arrested them."

"He'd have been at the house to get the reward if he had," rejoined Rob.

"Very well, then. He didn't catch them, and if the Hunts are at Aquebogue, that's where they've gone."

"Yes, but what's to prevent them leaving there?"

"No train after ninethirty till tomorrow morning, and the eight o'clock from here doesn't get to Aquebogue till after that time; so they must be stranded there, unless they have a car."

"Cookies and cream cakes! That's right!" cried Tubby, "let's phone the police at Aquebogue to look out for them."

But the lads found that the wire between Hampton and Aquebogue wasn't working. The telegraph office was closed. They exchanged blank glances.

"What are we going to do?" demanded Tubby.

"What all good scouts ought to dothe best we can,"rejoined Rob.

"And that is, under the present circumstances?" questioned Merritt.

"To go to our garageBlenkinsop'son Main Street, and get out the car."

"It'll be closed," rejoined Tubby.

"I've got a key," replied Rob; "I'll 'phone the house that I'm going for a night spin. We can get there, notify the police, and be back in two hours."

"Forward, scouts!" ordered Merritt, in sharp, "paradeground" tones, "and 'Be Prepared' for whatever comes along."

Rob found that the telephone to his home was also out of order, owing to repairs which were being rushed through by night. So ten minutes later, when the car glided out of the garage on Main Street and slipped silently through the sleeping town, there was nobody in Hampton who knew the Boy Scouts' night mission.

CHAPTER V.

A MIDNIGHT AUTO DASH.

The auto, a fast and heavy machine, plunged along through the night at a great rate. Its bright searchlight cast a brilliant circle of radiance far ahead into the darkness. Occasionally frightened birds could be seen flying out of the inky hedges, falling bewildered in the path of the white glare.

It was exhilarating, bloodstirring work, all the more keenly delightful from the sense of adventure with which it was spiced.

Rob was at the wheel, steering straight and steady. He knew the road well. Part of it had been the scene of that thrilling night ride described in The Boy Scouts and the Army Airship, when the boys had overtaken the two thieves who had stolen the aeroplane documents. On that occasion, it will be recalled, an accident had been narrowly averted by a soulstirring hair's breadth, as a train dashed across the tracks.

Rob's three companions sat back in the tonneau and conversed in low tones. Only the irrepressible Tubby was not duly impressed with the momentousness of the occasion. From time to time a snicker of laughter showed that he was cracking jokes in the same old way.

"Say," he remarked, as they bumped across the railroad tracks, "even if we do find out where these fellows are, I don't know just what we're going to do with them at this time of night. Reminds me"

"Oh, for goodness' sake, Tubby," groaned Merritt.

"Let him go ahead," struck in Hiram, "the sooner he blows off all his steam the sooner he'll shut up for good."

"Reminds me," went on the unruffled Tubby, "of what a little girl said to her mother when the kid asked her what sardines were. The mother explained that they were small fish that big ones ate. Then the little girl wanted to know how the big fish got them out of the tins."

There was a deathly silence, broken only by a low groan from Merritt.

"Call that a joke?" he moaned.

"Don't spring any more. My life ain't insured, by heck," put in Yankee Hiram.

"Well, that got a laugh in the minstrel show where I heard it," responded the aggrieved jokesmith.

Before long, lights flashed ahead of them, and, descending a steepish hill, they chugged into the town of Aquebogue. It was a fairly large town, and here and there lighted windows showed that some of the low resorts were still open for business. Far down the street shone two green lights, which marked the police station. The auto glided up to this, and Rob jumped out, accompanied by Merritt, leaving Tubby and Hiram in the car.

"Let's get out and stretch our legs a bit," said Tubby presently. It was taking some time for Rob to explain his errand to a sleepy police official.

"All right, my boy," drawled Hiram. "I'm not averse to a bit of legstretching."

The two lads got out and strolled as far as the street corner.

"H's'h!" exclaimed Tubby suddenly, as they reached it. He seized Hiram's arm with every appearance of excitement.

"Waal, what is it now?" asked the downeast boy; "more jokes and didoes?"

"No. See that chap just sneaking down the street from the opposite corner?"

"Yes; what of it? Are you seeing things?"

"No. But it's Freeman HuntI'm sure of it."

"By ginger, I believe you are right! It does look like him, for a fact. But what can he be doing here?"

"I've no more idea than you. But he must be up to some mischief."

"Reckon that's right."

"I tell you that where Freeman Hunt is, his father is not far off, and the rest of the gang must be about here, too. I guess it was a good thing we came out here."

"Well, what shall we do? Go back and tell the police?"

"No. While we were gone he'd sneak away, and we might miss him altogether. I've got a better plan."

"Do tell!"

"We'll follow him at a distance and see where he goes. Then we can come back and report."

"Saay, that's a good idea. Come on."

Freeman Hunt was almost out of sight now. But as the two scouts took up the trail, they saw him pause where a flood of light streamed from the window of a drinkingplace. He paused here for an instant and gave a low whistle; presently the boys' hearts gave a bound. From the doors of the resort issued three figures, one of which they recognized, even at that distance, as Stonington Hunt. With him were the two men who had played such a prominent part in the filching of the wallet belonging to Major Dangerfield.

"Keep in the shadow," whispered Tubby, crouching in a convenient doorway; "they haven't seen us. Hullo, there they go. Keep a good distance behindas far back as we can, without losing them."

The men the scouts were trailing struck into a lively pace. They seemed to be conversing earnestly. Through the shadows the two boys crept along behind them. Presently they were traversing a residence street, edged with elms and lawns and white picket fences. It was deserted and silent. The occupants of the houses were wrapped in sleep.

"Maybe they're going to turn into one of these houses," whispered Hiram.

But the men didn't. Instead, they kept right on, and before long the last electric light had been passed and they were in the open country.

"Hadn't we better turn back?" murmured Hiram. "It looks as if we were going too far for safety."

"Let's keep on," urged Tubby. "There's no danger. If we gave up the chase now we'd have had all our work for nothing."

Hiram made no reply, and the two boys, taking advantage of every bit of coveras the game of "Hare and Hounds" had taught themkept right on dogging the footsteps of their quarry. All at once Tubby began sniffing the air.

"We're getting near the sea," he proclaimed. "I can smell the salt meadows."

Aquebogue lay some distance back from the open waters of the ocean. It was situated, like Hampton itself, on an inlet. In the dim light of the stars, the two boys presently perceived that they were traversing a sort of dyke or raised road leading across the marshes.

"Where can they be going?" wondered Hiram.

"Don't know. But there are lots of fishermen's huts and shacks dotted about in the marshes. Maybe they are making for one of them."

"Maybe," opined Hiram, "but if you weren't so allsot on following them, I'd be in a good mind to turn back."

"Not yet," persisted Tubby, and the chase continued.

But it was soon to end. All at once the faint glimmer of a watercourse, or inlet from the sea, shone dimly in front of them. Upreared, too, against the starspangled sky, they could see the inky outlines of a structure of some kind.

"Crouch down here," said Tubby suddenly, as the men ahead of them came to a halt.

A bunch of marsh grass offered a convenient hiding place, and behind it the two boys lay flat. Pretty soon they heard the scratch of a match, and then the grating of a lock, as the door of the dark building they had remarked was opened. The men entered the place and slammed the door to. A few instants later, from the solitary window of the shack, a light shone out. The window was toward the creek, and the glare from it showed the two watching boys the mast and rigging of a large sloop. At least, from her spars, they judged her to be of considerable size.

"Gee whiz!" exclaimed Tubby, "we've found the place, all right. They must have come in that sloop. Maybe that's the way the two men who took the wallet got out of Hampton unobserved."

"But the wind's against the sloop, and she couldn't have beaten her way down here in that time," objected Hiram.

"She might have an engine, mightn't she?" whispered Tubby in scornful tones.

"That's so. Lots of boats do have gasoline motors. I guess you're right, Tubby. What are you going to do now? Go back?"

"Not much," rejoined the fat boy. "We'll just have a look into that hut and see what's going on. We might even get a chance to get that wallet back."

"Say, you're not going to take such a chance! If you looked through that window"

"Did I say I was going to look through the window, stupid? Don't you see that chimney on the roof? Now, the roof comes down low, almost to the ground. I'm going to climb up on it, and, by leaning over the chimney, I can hear what is said."

"But they'll hear your feet on the roof," objected the practical Hiram.

"I'm going to take my shoes off."

"It's awfully risky, Tubby."

"Say, look here, Hiram," sputtered the fat boy, "if this country was to go to war, you'd want to go to the front and fight for Old Glory as a Boy Scout, wouldn't you?"

"Of course."

"Well, then, don't you suppose that if you were scouting after an enemy you'd have to take bigger chances than this?"

Hiram said no more. Kicking their shoes off, and leaving them by the grass hummock, the two boys crept forward as silently as two cats. In the yielding sand their feet made no noise.

As Tubby had surmised, at the rear of the house the roof came almost to the ground, for the sand was heaped up against that particular wall, being driven in big dunes by the winds off the ocean.

“Up with you,” whispered Tubby, giving Hiram a “boost.” The Yankee boy’s long legs carried him onto the roof in a jiffy. Then came Tubby. Already the two boys could hear below them the low hum of voices, Freeman Hunt’s sharp, boyish tones mingling with the bass drone of the elder men’s conversation.

The roof was formed of driftwood and old timbers, and was as easy to climb as a staircase. Before many seconds, the boys were at the chimney. With beating pulses and a heart that throbbed faster than was altogether comfortable, in spite of his easygoing disposition, Tubby raised himself and peered down the flue. It was of brick. But to his astonishment, as he peered over the edge, he found he had a clear view of the room below.

The chimney, as is often the case in rough dwellings, did not go all the way down to the floor. Instead, it was supported on two beams, so that, peering down it, the boy could command a view of the room below, just as if he had been looking down a telescope.

Round a table were seated Stonington Hunt, the two roughlooking men who had stolen the wallet, and Freeman Hunt. A smoky glass lamp stood on the rough box which served for a table. Spread out on the table, too, was something that almost made Tubby let go his hold of the chimney and go sliding down the roof. It was the wallet, and beside it lay the paper covered with figures and markings, which, the boy had no doubt, was the precious document of the major.

“We’ll have to get out of here early in the morning,” Stonington Hunt was saying. “I don’t fancy having the police on my heels.”

“No. And Jim here says that those pesky Boy Scouts are mixed up in the search for the wallet,” struck in Freeman Hunt.

“Well, this is the time we give those brats the slip,” growled his father. “Come on, let’s turn in. We’ll get the motor going and drop down the creek before daylight.”

“Better leave the light burning then,” said one of the men who had been in Hampton that afternoon.

This was done, and presently snores and heavy breathing showed the men were asleep. Tubby could not see what resting places they had found, but assumed that there must be bunks around the edge of the hut, as is usual in such fishermen's shelters.

Before retiring, the men had shoved the paper into the wallet, but for some reason, probably they didn't think of it during their preparations for sleep, the wallet had been left on the table. It was almost directly below the chimney. As Tubby looked at it, he had a sudden idea.

"Got a bit of wire, Hiram?" he asked, knowing that the mechanical genius of the Eagle Patrol usually carried such odds and ends with him.

"Guess I've got a bit of brass wire right here," rejoined Hiram, "but it isn't very long."

"Long enough," commented Tubby, scrutinizing the bit handed to him, "now, if you had some string"

"Got a bit of fish line."

"Couldn't be better. Give it to me."

Much mystified, Hiram watched the fat boy bend the bit of wire and tie it to the string.

"Going fishing?" he asked in a sarcastic tone.

"Yes," replied Tubby quite seriously.

His quick eye had noted that the straps that closed the wallet had not been placed round it but lay in a loose loop on the table. If only he could entangle his improvised line in the loop, it would be an easy matter to fish up the wallet. If only he could do it!

Very cautiously, for he knew the risk he was running, Tubby lowered his line. Then he waited. But the breathing below continued steady and stentorian. Swinging his hook, which was quite heavy, the stout boy grappled cautiously for the wallet. It was tantalizing and delicate work. But after taking an infinity of pains, he finally succeeded in getting it fast.

Tubby at this moment had difficulty in suppressing a shout of "hooray!" But he mastered his emotions, and slowly and delicately began to haul in his "catch." Hiram, fascinated, crept close to his side. Perhaps it was this fact that was responsible for the disaster that occurred the next instant.

Without the slightest warning, save a sharp, cracking sound, the roof caved in under their feet. In a flash, both boys were projected in a heap into the room below. As they hurtled through the rotten covering of the hut, shouts and cries resounded from the aroused occupants.

CHAPTER VI.

IN DIREST PERIL.

The wildest confusion ensued. Fortunately, the drop was a short one, and beyond a few scratches and bruises, neither boy was hurt. The lamp, by some strange fatality, was not put out, but rolled off the table. As Stonington Hunt sprang at him, Tubby seized it. He brandished it threateningly.

"The Boy Scouts!" shouted Stonington Hunt, the first to recover from his stupefaction at the sudden interruption to their slumbers.

He dashed at Tubby, who swung the lamp for an instantit was his only weaponand then dashed it, like a smoky meteor, full at the advancing man's head.

It missed him by the fraction of an inch, or he would have been turned into a living torch.

Crash!

The lamp struck the opposite wall, and was shattered into a thousand fragments. Instantly the place was plunged in darkness, total and absolute. At the same instant a sharp report sounded. It seemed doubly loud in the tiny place. The fumes of the powder filled it reekingly.

"Don't shoot!" roared Stonington Hunt. "Guard the door and window. Don't let them get away."

"All right, dad," the boys heard Freeman Hunt cry loudly, as he scuffled across the room.

"Keep the doorway and the window," shouted Stonington Hunt. "I'll have a light in a jiffy. We've got them like two rats in a cage."

As he struck a match and lit a boat lantern that stood on a shelf, a low groan came from one corner of the room. Hiram was horrified to perceive that it was Tubby who uttered it. The shot must have wounded him, fired at haphazard, as it had been. The man who had aimed it, the bearded member of the gang, stood grimly by the doorway.

Almost beside himself at the hopelessness of their situation, Hiram gazed about him. All at once he noticed that on Tubby's chest a crimson stain was slowly spreading. The stout boy lay quite still except for an occasional quiver and groan. Without a thought as to his danger, Hiram disregarded Stonington Hunt's next injunction: "Don't move a step."

Swiftly he crossed to his wounded comrade. He sank on his knees beside him.

"TTTTubby," he exclaimed, "are you badly hurt, old man?"

To his amazement, the recumbent Tubby gave him a swift but knowing wink, and then, rolling over on his side again, resumed his groaning once more. Mystified, but comforted, Hiram was rising, when a rough hand seized him and sent him spinning to an opposite corner. It was the burly form of the bearded man that had propelled him.

"Not so rough, Jim Dale," warned Stonington Hunt. "We've got them where they can't escape. Lots of time to get what we want out of them."

"The pesky young spies," snorted Jim Dale, "I wonder how much they overheard of what we said."

"It don't matter, anyhow," put in his beardless companion of the afternoon. "They won't have no chance to tell it."

"Guess that's right, Pete Bumpus," struck in the bearded man. Suddenly Hiram felt a stinging slap across the face. He turned and faced young Freeman Hunt.

"How do you like that, eh?" snarled the youth viciously. "Here is where I pay you out for what you Scout kids did to me when we lived in Hampton."

He was stepping forward to deliver another blow, when Hiram ducked swiftly, and put into execution a maneuver Rob had shown him. As Freeman, a bigger and heavier lad, rushed forward, Hiram's long leg and his long left arm shot out simultaneously. The leg engaged Freeman's ankle, and the Yankee lad's fist encountered the other's chin with a sharp crack. Freeman Hunt fell in a heap on the floor. Hiram braced himself for an attack by the whole four. But it didn't come. Instead, they seemed to think it a good joke.

"That will teach you to keep your temper," laughed the boy's father roughly; "plenty of time to punch him and pummel him when we have them tied up."

“Maybe I won’t do it, too,” promised Freeman, gathering himself up, with a crestfallen look.

Stonington Hunt stepped up to Hiram.

“Tell me the truth, you young brat,” he snarled; “are the police after us?”

Hiram pondered an instant before answering. Then he decided on a course of action. Possibly it was a bad one, judging by the immediate results.

“Yes, they are,” he said boldly, “and if you don’t let us loose, you’ll get in trouble.”

Stonington Hunt paused irresolutely. Then he said:

“Get the sloop ready, boys. We’ll get out of here on the jump.”

A few moments later Hiram’s hands were bound and he was led on board the craft the boys had noticed lying in the creek. A plank connected it with the shore. Tubby, still groaning, was carried on board and thrown down in the bow beside Hiram.

“We’ll attend to him after a while,” said Hunt brutally; “if he’s badly wounded it’s his own fault, for meddling in other folks’ affairs.”

One of the men went below. Presently there came a sharp chugchug, and the anchor being taken in, the sloop began to move off down the creek. As Tubby Hopkins had surmised, she had an engine. Hunt, Jim Dale and Peter Bumpus stood in the bow. Hiram leaned disconsolately against a stay, and Tubby lay at his feet on a coil of rope.

The shores slipped rapidly by, and pretty soon the creek began to widen.

Freeman Hunt was at the wheel, and from time to time Jim Dale shouted directions back at him.

“Portport! Hard over!” or again, “Hard over! Starboard! There’s a shoal right ahead!”

A moon had risen now, and in the silvery light the darker water of the shoals, of which the creek seemed full, showed plainly.

"This crik's as full of sandbars as a hound dorg is uv fleas," grunted Jim Dale. "It won't be full tide for two hours or more, either. If"

There came a sudden, grinding jar.

"Hard over! Hard over!" bellowed Jim Dale.

Freeman Hunt spun the wheel like a squirrel in its cage. But it was too late. The sloop had grounded hard and fast. Leaving Peter Bumpus to guard the boys, Jim Dale and the elder Hunt leaped swiftly aft. They backed the motor, but it was no use. The sloop was too hard aground to be gotten off till the water rose.

"Two hours to wait till the tide rises," grumbled Jim Dale; "just like the luck."

Slowly the time passed. But never for an instant was the watch over the boys relaxed. Tubby lay still, and Hiram, almost carried out of himself by the rapid rush of recent events, leaned miserably against the stay.

At last, just as a faint, gray light began to show in the east, they could feel the sloop moving under their feet. With reversed motor, she was backed off the sandbar, or mudshoal, and the journey resumed. As the light grew stronger, Hiram saw that they were dropping rapidly down toward the sea. Right ahead of them could now be seen the white foam and spray, where the breakers of the open sea were shattering themselves on the bar at the mouth of the creek.

The channel was narrow and intricate, but Jim Dale, who seemed to be a good pilot, and who had assumed the wheel, brought the sloop through it in safety. Before long, under her keel could be felt the long lift and drive of the open Atlantic.

By gazing at the sun, Hiram saw that the sloop's head was pointed west. By this he judged that her navigators meant to head down the Long Island shore toward New York.

The sunrise was red and angry. Hiram, with his knowledge of scoutlore, knew that this presaged bad weather. But the crew of the sloop did not seem to notice it. After a while they began to make preparations to hoist sail, as the breeze was freshening.

"Take those kids below," ordered Stonington Hunt suddenly. Under the escort of Jim Dale, who had relinquished the wheel to Freeman Hunt and Pete Bumpus, the ladsTubby being carriedwere presently installed in a small, dark cabin in the stern of the sloop. This done, the companionway door was closed, and they heard a key grate in a lock. They were prisoners, then, at sea, on this mysterious sloop?

"What next?" groaned Hiram to himself, sinking down on a locker.

"Why, I guess the next thing to do is for me to come to life, my valiant downeaster," cried Tubby, springing erect from the corner into which he had been thrown. The apparently badly wounded lad seemed as active and chipper as ever.

CHAPTER VII.

ADRIFT IN THE STORM.

At the same instant the sloop staggered and heeled over, sending Hiram half across the dingy cabin. He caught at a stanchion and saved himself. Then he turned his amazed gaze afresh on Tubby. The stout youth stood by the companion stairs, regarding him with a grin. Presently he actually began to hum:

"A life on the ocean wave!
A home on the rolling deep!
"Yo ho, my hearties," he added, with a nautical twitch at his breeches, "we're going to have a rough day of it."

As if in answer, the sloop heeled over to another puff. A tin dish, dislodged from the rusty stove, went clattering across the inclined cabin floor. But still Hiram stood gaping vacantly at Tubby.

"Well, what's the matter?" inquired that individual cheerfully, "have you lost that voice of yours?"

"No, bbbbut I thought you were badly wounded!" Hiram managed to sputter.

"No, bbbbut I thought you were badly wounded!" Hiram managed to sputter.
"No, bbbbut I thought you were badly wounded!" Hiram managed to sputter.

"So I was, but in reverse English only," said Tubby cheerfully; "the bullet just nicked me and knocked the breath out of me for a minute. When I came to, I saw that the best thing I could do was to act like Br'er Rabbit and lay low."

Hiram looked his admiration.

"Waal," he drawled, dropping, as he seldom did even in emotional moments, into his New England dialect, "ef you ain't ther beatingist!

"But, say," he added quickly, "what about that red stain on your shirt? Look, it's all over the front of your uniform."

“Jiggeree, so it is. I guess that fountain pen of mine must have been busted cold by that bullet. I had it filled with red ink, because I’d been helping Rob fill out some reports to mail to Scout headquarters. Ho! ho!” the fat boy broke into open mirth, “it certainly does look as if some one had tapped my claret. Yoho! that was a corker!”

The sloop lurched and dipped deeper than ever. They could see the green water obscure the port hole for an instant.

“That sea’s getting up right along,” said Tubby presently, as he unbound Hiram’s hands. “Say, Hiram,” he added anxiously, “you don’t get seasick easily, do you?”

“Nnnno, that is, I don’t think so,” sputtered Hiram rather dubiously.

“Well, don’t, I beg from my heart! Don’t get seasick till we get on land again.”

“I’ll try not to,” said the downeast boy seriously, ignoring the fine “bull” which Tubby’s remark contained.

“Reminds me,” said Tubby presently, “of what the sea captain said to the nervous lady. She went up to him and told him that her husband was scared of getting seasick. ‘My husband’s dreadfully liable to seasickness, captain,’ she said. ‘What must I tell him to do if he feels it coming on?’ ‘You needn’t tell him anything, ma’am,’ said the captain; ‘no need to tell him what to dohe’ll do it.’”

But somehow this bit of humor did not bring even a wan smile to Hiram, willing as he usually was to laugh at Tubby’s whimsical jokes. Instead, he turned a pale face on his companion.

“IIdo feel pretty bad, for a fact!” he moaned.

“Oh, Jiminy Crickets!” wailed Tubby, “he’s going to be seasick!”

Hiram, with a ghastly face of a greenishyellow hue, sank down on one of the lockers, resigning himself to his fate. The sloop began to plunge and tumble along in a more lively fashion than ever. Overhead Tubby could hear the trample of feet, as her crew ran about trying to weather the blow.

Suddenly, above the howling of the wind, Tubby heard a sharp click at the companionway door. The next instant the companionway slide was shoved back and a gust of fresh, saltladen air blew into the close cabin. Stonington Hunt's form was on the stairway the next moment, and Tubby, with a quick dive, threw himself on the floor in a corner, carrying out once more his rôle of the badly wounded scout.

Lying there, and breathing in a quick, distressed way, Tubby, out of the corner of his eye, watched the man as he moved about. Hunt's first idea was evidently to rouse Hiram. Perhaps he needed him to help in navigating the stormbuffeted craft. But he soon gave up the task of instilling the seasick lad with ambition or life. Then came Tubby's turn, but after bending over the fat boy for an instant, Hunt muttered:

"He's no good," and without offering to aid the supposedly injured boy, moved away. He ascended the steps and presently the companion slide banged to, and the padlock clicked once more.

Tubby arose, as soon as he was convinced the coast was clear, and, despairing of arousing Hiram, sat on a locker and began to think hard. Rather bitterly he went over in his mind the circumstances leading to their present predicament. In the first place, he could not but own he had had no business to embark on such an enterprise at all without a bigger force. In the second place, if he had lived up to the Scouts' motto of "Be Prepared," there was a strong possibility that they would not have been so disastrously precipitated through the roof of the lonely hut. However, before long, Tubby's naturally buoyant temperament asserted itself. As became a boy who had won a firstclass scoutship, he did not waste any further time on vain regrets. Instead of crying over spilled milk, he began to figure on finding a way out of their predicament.

Casting his eyes about the cabin, he suddenly became aware of a small door in the bulkhead at the forward end of it. Curious by nature, Tubby opened it, and peered into a dark, cavernous space. A strong odor of gasoline saluted his nostrils, and presentlyhis eyes becoming used to the lighthe could make out the occasional glint of metal. In a flash he realized that this was the engineroom of the sloop, and housed her auxiliary motor.

A buttonswitch being made out by the boy at this moment, he turned it. Instantly two incandescent lights shone out, illuminating the place. By their light Tubby made out another door beyond the motor. Determined to investigate the sloop thoroughlycome what mighthe thrust it open, and found himself in what seemed to be the hold. But it was too dark to perceive much. Besides, the sloop was pitching and rolling so terribly that the lad had all he could do to hold on.

Returning to the engineroom, he almost stumbled across an electric torch secured to a bracket on the bulkhead. It was evidently used for examining the motor without exposing an open light to the fumes of the gasoline. Armed with this, Tubby once more investigated the hold. It was a capacious place. Stanchions, like a forest of bare trees, supported the deck above. So far as the boy could make out, the place was empty. Far forward was a ladder leading up to a hatchway. Tubby, following out his naturally inquiring bent of mind, was about to examine this, when his heart gave a great bound and then stood still.

He had not thought to cast a glance behind him in his eagerness to examine the hold.

This had proved to be a fatal bit of oversight on his part, for Stonington Hunt and his son, descending to the cabin for some purpose, had observed his absence. A brief investigation showed them the open door into the engineroom and thence they had glimpsed the flash of Tubby's torch.

The boy turned, warned by some instinct, just as they tiptoed up behind him. Freeman Hunt, with a grin on his face, rushed straight at the Boy Scout. But Tubby was prepared this time, at any rate. He dashed the torch, end down, on the floor of the hold, extinguishing it instantly. At almost the same instant, he rushed straight at the place where he had last seen Freeman Hunt.

To his huge satisfaction, he felt the other go down in a sprawling heap under his onrush. As he fell, Freeman gave a shout of:

"He ain't wounded at all, dad! He was fooling us!"

"Yes, the brat! He was!" shouted Stonington Hunt, blundering about in the black hold and striving to keep his footing on the pitching, heaving floor.

Tubby, guided by instinct, dashed forward toward the spot, as nearly as he could judge its location, where he had noticed the ladder. He found it, and had placed his foot on the bottom rung, when there was a sudden shock.

The motion of the sloop seemed to cease, as if by magic. Tubby felt himself hurled forward into darkness by the shock. His head crashed against something, and a world of brilliant constellations swam in a glittering array before his eyes. Then something in his head seemed to give way with a snap, and young Hopkins knew no more.

CHAPTER VIII.

EAGLES ON THE TRAIL.

"Hullo! Wonder what's become of those two fellows?"

Merritt voiced the inquiry, as he and Rob emerged from the police station. The sergeant in charge had promised to do all he could to apprehend the stealers of the pocketbook if they were anywhere within striking distance of Aquebogue.

Rob looked about him. There stood the automobile. But of the two lads they had left to guard it there was no sign. After waiting a reasonable time, the two Boy Scout leaders began to feel real alarm.

"Somehow I feel as if Hunt and his gang have got something to do with this," murmured Rob uneasily.

"It does seem queer," admitted Merritt. "Let's look around a bit more, and then, if we find no trace of them, we'll go back to the police station and look for aid."

"All right; I guess that's the best thing to do."

But, as we know, it was impossible that their search could terminate in anything but failure. Not a little worried, Rob informed their friend, the sergeant, of what had occurred. That official at once galvanized into action. Before this, he had not seemed to take much interest in their affairs. But now he really moved quickly. By telephone he summoned two detectives, and the lads soon put them in possession of the facts in the case.

"Pretty slim grounds to work on," remarked one of them with a shrug.

Rob could not but feel that this was true. After their consultation with the detectives, who at once set out to scour the place for some trace of Hunt and his crew, the two lads, much dispirited, and with heavy hearts, set out for home. They arrived there in the early morning, and turned in for a brief sleep. As Rob had expected, his father was not at all pleased when he learned of the nocturnal use made of his car, and of the serious consequences which had ensued. But Major Dangerfield, who had listened to the lad's story with interestit was related at the breakfast tablewas inclined to take a less serious view of the matter.

"After all, Mr. Blake," he said, "the boys behaved like true Boy Scouts. It was their duty to try to aid in the matter of the pocketbook, and they did their best. I think that it was cleverly done, too."

"But young Hopkins and Hiram are missing," protested Mrs. Blake. "What will their parents say?"

"I don't think, from my observation of Master Hopkins, that he is the kind of lad to get into serious difficulties," said the major. "In fact, I am convinced that he has stumbled across some clew and is following it up."

"I hope it may be so, and that both of them are safe," said Mrs. Blake fervently.

The first duty, after the morning meal, was to call on Mrs. Hopkins, who was a widow, and also on Hiram's parents, and explain the case. It was not a pleasant task, but Rob saw it through with Spartan courage. He succeeded in quelling the first vivid alarm of the lads' parents, however, and promised to return with news of them before the day was over. This done, Major Dangerfield, Merritt and Rob set out in the Blake car for Aquebogue.

"It is your duty as Boy Scouts to find your missing comrades," said Mr. Blake, as the car started off.

"We'll do it, if it's possible" began Merritt dolefully.

"We'll do it, anyway," said Rob stoutly.

"That's the right Scout way to talk," said the major commendingly, "that is the spirit that will win."

No news greeted them on their arrival in Aquebogue. The two detectives were still out on the case, and the officials in charge had nothing to report. This was discouraging, but before long one of the detectives arrived with an important clew. He carried in his hand a paper package. On being opened, it proved to contain two pairs of shoes, of Boy Scout pattern. Rob and Merritt immediately identified them as belonging to Hiram and young Hopkins. The major seemed much impressed by the value of this bit of evidence, and before many minutes had passed they were all in the auto and spinning toward the spot where the articles of apparel had been discovered.

The detectives, it transpired, had not yet explored the hut, and Rob's keen eyes were the first to spy the jagged hole in its roof. He at once set his scout training to work. The first thing he observed was that the hole had been freshly torn. An investigation of the inside of the hut showed the traces of the fight between Hiram and young Hunt.

All at once Rob gave a sharp exclamation, and pounced on some object in a corner of the place. Its bright glitter, as the light fell on it through the hole in the roof, had attracted him at first. True Scout as he was, Rob did not allow even the minutest object to escape his scrutiny. In this case, he was richly rewarded, for what he had seen turned out to be a Scout button. It was one that had been torn from Hiram's coat in the struggle.

"This is conclusive evidence that the two lads were here," decided the major. "What else can you deduce from what you have seen, Rob?"

The leader of the Eagle Patrol pondered a moment. Then he spoke.

"In the first place," he said decidedly, "it is evident that Tubby and Hiram in some way got on the track of our enemies in the town. They followed them here. That is proved by the finding of their shoes on that dune near the hut. They took their shoes off for some object, of course. Evidently it must have been to silently observe the men who occupied this shanty. By looking at the footmarks in the sand outside, I traced them to the wall of the place. The steps did not turn in at the door, therefore, obviously, they must have climbed on the roof, for the steps ended at the lowhanging eaves, and they do not go back.

"An examination of the roof shows that it must have given way under their combined weight. See, that beam is as brittle as matchwood, from dry rot. They could not have been hurtat least, I don't think soor this button, which must have been torn off in a struggle, for they are tightly sewn on, would not have been found."

"Very good," approved the major. "I have seen Indian scouts on the border who could not have done much better. But what is the next step?"

"To find out what has become of them, of course," put in Merritt.

"Well, let's see how close we can come to deciding that," said the major, with a side glance at the detectives, who seemed puzzled and bewildered at the swift deductive work of the young Scout.

Merritt left the hut and made a hasty examination of the numerous tracks without. He then scrutinized the muddy banks of the inlet closely. The tide was not yet full, and the marks of the sloop's keel still showed. Also sand had been tracked on to the little wharf. It was evident that a vessel of some sort had lain there between tides. Equally plain did it appear, that the two missing lads had been carried on board her. Merritt lost no time in communicating his discoveries to his companions.

"You have done well," commended the former army officer, "I am convinced that your deductions are, in the main, correct. But now the thing is to get some craft to go in pursuit of these fellows."

"Ike Menjes, up the creek a little way, has a big gasoline launch he lets out," volunteered one of the detectives.

"We'll get it if possible," said the major instantly. "Is she a fast boat?"

"None quicker hereabouts," said the other arm of the law.

Ten minutes later a bargain had been struck, and with Ike Menjes at the engine, and Rob at the wheel, the swift launch Algonquin was dashing off down the winding creek headed for the open sea. As she tumbled and rolled through the rough waters of the bar at the creek's mouth, Rob's eye swept the sky.

"Bad weather coming," he remarked.

"No need to worry in this craft," declared Ike; "she's weathered the worst we ever get off here."

"I expect so," agreed the major, with an approving glance at the craft's broad lines and generous beam.

Before many moments had passed, Rob's prediction came true. The Algonquin, without any diminution of speed, was being pushed along through a rapidly rising sea, while the wind howled about her, growing stronger every moment. Rob caught himself wondering what sort of a craft the kidnappers of the boys possessed. He hoped it was staunch, for in his judgment the blow was going to be a bad one.

"It'll get worser before it gets betterer," opined Ike Menjes, coming forward from his engines and peering ahead at the tumbling masses of green water. The rising wind caught their tops and feathered them off in masses of snowy spume. Overhead, dark, ragged clouds raced along. So low did they hang that they seemed almost to touch the crests of the angry waves.

Each time the Algonquin topped a roller and then staggered down into a deep trough, Rob scanned the surrounding sea eagerly. But no sign, had, so far, appeared, of any craft resembling the one which they knew must have left the creek. Seaward some sails showed, but they were all those of large coasting schooners.

The craft they were in search of was, no doubt, a smallish vessel, otherwise she could not have negotiated the narrow, winding creek, with its innumerable bends and shallow places.

"Keep more in shore," advised Ike. "They may have hugged the land to get the benefit of the weather shore."

Rob headed closer in toward the lowlying coast. He could see the waves breaking angrily in white masses on the sandy beach. All at once, above a distant point of land, he sighted the gray shoulder of a sail. The next instant it had vanished.

Had it found an opening through which to slip into an inlet in the bleak coast, or had it foundered in the wild breakers?

The question agitated Rob hugely. Some intuition told him that the craft he had glimpsed had been the one they were in search of, but of its fate they could have no immediate knowledge.

CHAPTER IX.

WHAT SCOUT HOPKINS DID.

When young Hopkins came to himself, he was dimly conscious that the driving motion of the sloop had ceased. Instead, lying there in the pitchy darkness of the hold, he could feel the vessel being struck with what appeared to be mighty blows from a Titanic hammer. Tubby guessed instantly, from the sensations, that they were aground, and that what he felt was the terrific bombardment of enormous breakers.

A swift "overhauling" of himself soon showed the lad that he was not hurt, although the blow on his head, when he had been hurled from the ladder, had stunned him. Of how long he had been unconscious, he had, of course, no knowledge. Worse still, he could not form any idea of how to get out of his dark prison, and he realized that he had no time to lose if he wanted to save Hiram and himself.

Risking the chance that their enemies were prowling about, waiting for the lad to declare himself, Tubby set up a shout.

"Hiram! Oh, Hiram!"

In the intervals of the crashing blows that shook the frail sloop from stem to stern, Tubby listened intently. But for some time no answering cry came to greet him. Then all at once he thought he caught a feeble shout. He responded, and the cry came more distinctly. Guided by it, he made his way aft with considerable difficulty. Presently a dim, gray light, filtering through the blackness, apprised him that he was nearing the door in the bulkhead through which he had blundered into the hold. A moment more and he had passed through the engineroom and was in the cabin. Hiram, looking pale and wild, was clinging to a stanchion. Water had come into the cabin through a broken port, and was washing about the floor.

"Oh, Tubby, I'm so glad you've come. Where have you been?" breathed the unfortunate Hiram, weak and shaky from his bout with seasickness. "What is happening?"

"I guess we're aground somewhere," rejoined Tubby. "I'm going to see."

He made for the companionway and rattled the door at the top. As he had dreaded, it was locked. They were prisoners on board a doomed vessel. For an instant even young Hopkins' resourcefulness came to a standstill. His heart seemed to stop beating. His head swam madly. Was this to be the end of them, to be drowned miserably, like two captive rats?

But the next instant the thought of their plight acted as a stimulus. “A true Scout should never say die,” thought the boy, and then, retracing his steps, he joined Hiram.

“What’s become of Hunt and his outfit?” he asked.

“Why, Stonington Hunt and Freeman passed through the cabin a few minutes ago,” replied Hiram, “right after that terrible bump”

“When the sloop struck,” thought Tubby. Aloud he said:

“Well?”

“I heard them say that you were done for, and that I could be left to drown.”

“Yes, yes, Hiram; but did they say anything about escaping themselves?”

“Yes. I heard them shouting on deck to cut loose the boat. Then I heard a lot of noise. I guess they launched her. That’s all, till I heard you shouting back in there.”

“Humph!” ejaculated Tubby; “so they left us to perish on this old sloop, eh? Well, Hiram, we’ll fool ’em. We’ll get away yet in spite of them.” In talking thus, young Hopkins assumed a confidence he was far from feeling, but he deemed it best to stimulate Hiram with hope.

“Got any matches?” was his next question.

Hiram nodded, and presently handed out a box.

“Good. Now follow me. By the way, how’s the seasickness?”

“Oh, better, but I feel shaky yet. I can manage, though.”

“That’s the stuffwough!”

A heavier blow than usual had been dealt the sloop. The two lads could feel her quiver and quake under the concussion like a live thing.

"Come on, we've got to move quick," said Tubby. Striking a match, he set off into the hold. Hiram followed. Before long they stood at the foot of the ladder from which Tubby had been so violently flung a short time before.

The stout youth darted up it with an agility one would not have expected in a boy of his girth. With the strongest shove of which he was capable, he pushed up the scuttle above.

To his great joy, it gave, swinging back on hinges. But, as he opened it fully, Tubby came nearly being hurled from the ladder for the second time. A great mass of green water swept across the deck at that instant, and the full force of the torrent descended into the hole through the open hatch. Luckily, Tubby had seen it coming in time to warn Hiram, and the downeast lad clung on tightly enough to avoid being carried from his foothold.

In a jiffy young Hopkins clambered through, shouting to Hiram to follow him. It was a wild scene that met both boys' eyes when they emerged on the deck of the stranded sloop. She lay in a small inlet which, though partially sheltered, in hard storms was swept by the seas from outside. The sloop was heeled over to one side at so steep an angle that standing on her wet decks was impossible without clinging to something.

About three hundred yards away lay the shore, a wild, uninhabited expanse of windswept sand dunes, overgrown with dull, green and prickly beachgrass. No sign of a human habitation could be discerned. Outside on the beach the big seas thundered, flinging masses of white foam skyward. It seemed almost impossible that she could have been navigated through the narrow inlet leading into the small bay where she had stranded. As a matter of fact, it had been more by luck than by design that she had accomplished the passage.

All at once, as the two castaways stood looking about them, a figure bobbed up from behind one of the sand hills. It was instantly recognized by Tubby as Stonington Hunt. The lad now saw that a boat lay on the beach; evidently then, that was how they had reached the shore, as Hiram had surmised. Hunt had apparently been seeking shelter from the storm behind the dune, with the rest of his band. As his eyes fell on the figures of the two Boy Scouts standing on the deck of the stranded sloop, he beckoned toward the dune. Instantly there appeared the rest of the lads' enemies.

They stood staring for a few minutes, as if amazed to see the Boy Scouts. But before they had time to take any action, an astonishing thing happened.

The sloop began to move.

The incoming tide, which had been steadily rising, had floated her, and she gradually reeled off the sand bank, on which she had struck, into open water. As she did so, Tubby suddenly ducked low, and something whistled by his head. Above the wind came the crack of a firearm's report. Gazing toward Stonington Hunt, Tubby saw that the man held a revolver in his hand. It was from this weapon, evidently, that the projectile had been discharged.

"Get out of the way, Hiram, quick!" exclaimed the stout lad, for he now saw that the others were preparing to discharge pistols at them. It was apparent that they did not mean the boys to escape if they could avoid it.

But Tubby had suddenly thought of a plan. It had been born in his mind when the sloop rolled off the shoal into deep water. He knew something of gasoline engines from his experiences on board the Flying Fish. Why would it not be possible to get out of the little and dangerous bay under motor power? The shots hastened his decision. Clearly if they remained where they were, destruction swift and certain threatened. Stonington Hunt did not mean to let them land, so much was only too apparent.

Before the men left the sloop they had hauled down the canvas, probably in an effort to keep her from grounding. It was the work of an instant for Tubby to dash below and give a turn to the rear starting device on the engine. It worked perfectly. Then he turned on the gasolene, easily finding the connection, and threw on the switch. A blue spark showed that the current was on. Then, with a beating heart he turned the starting device once more.

Bang!

The engine moved. To the lad's delight it worked steadily. This done, he darted back on deck and took the wheel. He was not a moment too soon, for, with no one at the helm, the craft was heading once more for the sand bank. Crouching beneath the stern bulwarks, and ordering Hiram to do the same, young Hopkins navigated the sloop skilfully ahead, steering straight for the open sea. Tempestuous as it was, the sloop seemed still staunch, and he felt they were safer there than in such close proximity to Hunt. Especially since they were followed by an unceasing fire from the pistols of the gang. But although some of the shots splintered the bulwarks, sending showers of slivers about the two crouching lads, neither were hit.

At last, after a dozen hairraising escapes on the choppy bar, the sloop gained the outside, and throwing showers of spray high over her bluff bows, began to breast the sweep of the seas.

"Go below and take a look at the glass oil cups," ordered Tubby as soon as they were safe from the firing, "if any of them are empty fill them. There is an oil can on a shelf beside the motor."

Glad to do anything to help out, Hiram hastened on this errand. He was below about ten minutes. When he returned on deck his face was white, and he was breathing quickly. Tubby's quick eye noted, too, that the lad was wet to the waist.

"What's up below?" he demanded.

"The cabin's half full of water, and it seems to be rising every minute;" was the disquieting reply.

At the same instant the sloop's motion stopped and she began rolling in a sickening fashion in the troughs of the mighty seas.

"Jehoshaphat!" exclaimed Scout Hopkins, "we're in for it now. The water's reached the engine and it's stopped!"

As he spoke a gigantic mountain of green water suddenly towered right above the helpless sloop. Its crest seemed to overtop the mast tip. Automatically Tubby crouched low and reached out a hand for Hiram.

The next instant the wave swept down on them enveloping the lads in a turmoil of salt water. The two boys were swept away in the liquid avalanche like feathers before a gale.

When the wave had passed, the wreck of the sloop could be seen staggering and wallowing like a stricken thing. But of her two recent occupants there was no trace upon the wilderness of heaving waters.

CHAPTER X.

A RESCUE AND A BIVOUAC.

From the bow of the Algonquin Rob kept his eyes riveted on the spot at which he had seen the sloop vanish. But for some time he could see nothing but the billowing crests of the waves. Suddenly, to his astonishment, from the midst of the combing summits, there was revealed the swaying mast of the sloop, cutting great arcs dizzily across the lowering sky.

As the Algonquin climbed to a wave top the entire length of the sloop was disclosed to the lad's gaze. On her deck he could now plainly see two figures.

"Got a glass?" he inquired of Ike.

"Sure," responded that individual, floundering forward with a pair of binoculars.

Rob clapped them to his eyes. The figures of Hiram and Tubby Hopkins swam into the field of vision. At the same instant, or so it seemed, Rob made out the wall of green water rushing downward upon the sloop.

While a cry of alarm still quivered upon his lips, the sloop rallied an instant, and thenwas wiped out!

The others had pressed forward too, and the Algonquin had, by that time, gotten close enough for them all to witness the marine tragedy.

"Steady, Rob," exclaimed the major, his hand on Rob's shoulder, "they may be all right yet."

Rob's face was white and set, but he nodded bravely. It seemed impossible that anything living could have escaped from the overwhelming avalanche of water.

Merritt seized the glasses as Rob set them down to take the wheel again. He peered through them with straining eyes.

"Hullo, what's that off in the water there?" he shouted suddenly, pointing.

The next instant the object he had descried had vanished in the trough of a sea.

"Could you make out anybody?" asked the major anxiously.

"It looked like a spar withYes, there are two figures clinging to it."

"Here, let me look!" Rob snatched the glasses out of his comrade's hand.

"Hooray!" he cried the next instant, "it's Tubby and Hiram!"

"Are you sure?" asked the major, "perhaps it's some members of Hunt's crew."

"No, it's Tubby and Hiram. I can make out their uniforms," cried Rob. As he spoke he swung the wheel over, and the Algonquin's head was turned in the direction of the spot where a spar with two objects clinging to it had last been seen.

"Wonder what can have become of Hunt and his crowd?" said Merritt presently.

"Maybe they've met with a watery grave," conjectured one of the detectives, "and from what you've told me it would be a good end for them."

"If they hain't taken that pocketbook with them," put in his companion, "the kidnapping of those boys was as desperate a bit of work as I've ever heard tell of."

In a brief time the two lads, none the worse apparently for their immersion, had been hauled on board the Algonquin, and were being plied with eager questions.

"I guess I caught on to that boom more by instinct than anything else," explained Tubby, "when I got the water out of my lungs I looked about me and saw that Hiram had grabbed it too."

"That's what I call luck," said one of the detectives in a wondering tone.

"It surely was," agreed Hiram, "but I guess there's a bigger bit coming."

"What do you mean?" asked the major, struck by something odd in the lad's tone.

For answer Tubby thrust a hand into an inside pocket of his coat and drew forth something that, dripping with water as it was, could be easily recognized asthe missing pocketbook!

Tubby drew forth the missing pocketbook.
Tubby drew forth the missing pocketbook.

"I guess they forgot to search me for it in the excitement following the collapse of the roof. I'm sorry it got wet, major," he added.

But the major and the others could only regard the fat boy with wondering eyes. Suddenly the major, the first to recover his senses, spoke:

"I don't know how I'm ever to thank you for this, Hopkins," he began.

"Tell you how you can," spoke the irrepressible Tubby swiftly.

"How, my boy?"

"By taking us some place where we can get something to eat," quoth Tubby, "I'm so hungry I could demolish the left hind leg of a brass monkey without winking."

From the tumbling waves of an angry sea to the cool shadows of a magnificent forest of chestnut and oak may be a long distance to travel, but such is the jump over time and space that we must make if we wish to accompany our Boy Scouts to their Mountain Camp. The evening sun, already almost touching the peaks of the nearest range, was striking level shafts of light through the forest as our party came to a halt, and Major Dangerfield ordered the canoes, by which they had traversed the smooth stretches of Echo Lake, hauled ashore.

It was more than three days since the party had left the shores of Lake Champlain. The passage of the lake from its lower end had been made by canoes. The same craft they were now using had transported them. There were three of the frail, delicate little vessels. One was blue, another a rich Indian red, and the third a dark green.

The canoes had been purchased by Major Dangerfield at Lakehead, a small town at which they left the railroad. They had been stocked with provisions and equipment for their long dash into the solitudes of the Adirondacks. Reaching Dangerfield, the canoes had been transported overland till the first of a chain of lakes, leading into the interior, had been reached. Here, to the boys' huge delight, they once more took to the water.

In the party were Rob, Merritt, young Hopkins, Hiram and little Andy Bowles, the bugler of the Eagles. Andy had been brought along because, as Rob had said, he was so little he would tuck in anywhere. Of course there had been keen regret on the part of the lads who were, of necessity, left behind. But they had borne it with true scout spirit and wished their lucky comrades all the good fortune in the world, when they embarked from Hampton.

Travel had bronzed the lads and stained and crumpled their smart uniforms. But they looked very fit and scoutlike as they bustled about, making the various preparations for the evening's camp. Two members of the party have not yet been mentioned. One of these was a tall, lanky man with a pair of big hornrimmed spectacles set athwart his nose, and arrayed in a queer combination of woodsman's clothes and a pedant's immaculate dress. He had retained a white lawn tie and long black coat, but his nether limbs were encased in corduroys and gaiters, with a pair of big, squaretoed shoes protruding beneath. On his head was an oddlooking round, black hat, which was always getting knocked into the water or caught on branches and swept off. This queer figure was Professor Jeremiah Jorum.

The second addition to the party was the major's factotum, Christopher Columbus Julius Pompey Snaggs. But for purposes of identification he answered to the name of Jumbo. Jumbo was a bigframed negro, intensely black and with a sunny, childlike disposition. He had a propensity for coining words to suit his convenience, deeming the King's English insufficient in scope to express his emotions.

Standing on the sandy strip of beach as he emerged from the red canoe, with a load of "duffle," Jumbo gazed about him in an interested way.

"Dis sutt'in'ly am a glumpferiferous spot to locate a camp," he remarked, letting his big eyes roll from the tranquil expanse of lake, fringed with feathery balsams and firs, to the slope above him clothed in its growth of fine timber, some of it hundreds of years old.

"Here you, Jumbo, hurry up with that bedding and then clean those fish!"

The voice was the major's. It hailed from a level spot a short distance above the sandy beach. On this small plateau, the canvas "tepees" the Boy Scouts carried were already erected, and a good fire was burning between two green logs.

"Yas, sah, yas, sah! I'se a comin'," hailed the negro, lumbering up among the loose rock, and almost spilling his load in his haste, "I'se a coming so quintopulous dat you all kain't see muh fer de dus' I'se raisin'."

Before long the fish, caught by trolling as they came along, were frizzling in the pan, and spreading an appetizing odor abroad. The aroma of coffee and camp biscuit mingled with the other appetizing smells.

"Race anybody down to the lake for a wash!" shouted Rob suddenly.

In a flash he was off, followed by Merritt, Hiram and Tubby. Little Andy Bowles, with his bugle suspended from his shoulders by a cord of the Eagle colors, hurried along behind on his stumpy little legs.

"I win!" shouted Rob as he, with difficulty, paused on the brink of the lake. But hardly were the words out of his mouth before Merritt flashed up beside him.

"Almost a dead heat," laughed Rob, "IBut hullo, what's all this?"

Above them came a roar of sliding gravel and stones that sounded like an avalanche. In the midst of it was Tubby, his rotund form dashing forward at a great rate. His legs were flashing like the pistons of a racing locomotive as he plunged down the hillside.

"Here, stop! stop!" shouted Rob, "you'll be in the lake in a minute!"

But the warning came too late. Tubby's heavy weight could not be checked so easily. Faster he went, and faster, striving in vain to stop himself.

"He's gone!" yelled Merritt the next instant, as a splash announced that Tubby had plunged into the lake water.

In a flash the fat boy was on the surface. But he was "dead game," and while his comrades shouted with laughter he swam about, puffing like a big porpoise.

"Come on in, the water's fine," he exclaimed.

"Even with your uniform on?" jeered Hiram.

"Sure! Ohouch! what's that?"

The fat boy had perceived a queerlooking head suddenly obtrude from the water close to him. It was evident that he was not the only one to enjoy an evening swim that day. A big water snake was sharing his involuntary bath with him.

Tubby struck out with might and main for shore, and presently reached it, dripping profusely. The major, when he heard of the occurrence, ordered a change of clothes. When this had been made, Andy's bugle sounded the quick lively notes of the mess call, and the Boy Scouts and their elders gathered round the table which the boys' deft hands had composed of flat slabs of birch bark supported on trestles of green wood. They sat on camp stools which they carried with them. How heartily they ate! They had the appetites that are born of woods and open places.

"Mah goodness, dose boys mus' have stumicks lak der olyphogenius mammaothstikuscudsses!" exclaimed Jumbo as he hurried to and from his cooking fire in response to constant demands for "more."

CHAPTER XI.

THE MOUNTAIN CAMP.

Supper concluded, the talk naturally fell to the object of their expedition. The chart or map of the treasuretrove's location was brought out and pored over in the firelight, for the nights were quite sharp, and a big fire had been lighted.

"How soon do you think we will be within striking distance of the place?" inquired Rob.

"Within two or three days, I should estimate," replied the former officer, "but of course we may be delayed. For instance, we have a portage ahead of us."

"Aahow much?" asked Tubby.

"A portage. That means a point of land round which it would not be practicable to canoe. At such a place we shall have to take the canoes out of the water and carry them over the projection of land to the next lake."

"Anybody who wants it can have my share of that job," said Tubby, "I guess I'll delegate Andy Bowles to carry out my part."

There was a general laugh at the idea of what a comical sight the diminutive bugler would present staggering along under the weight of a canoe.

"Andy would look like a littleneck clam under its shell," chuckled Merritt.

"Well, you can't always gauge the quality of the goods by the size of the package they come in," chortled Andy, "look at Tubby, for instance. He"

But the fat boy suddenly projected himself on the little bugler. But Andy, though small, was tough as a roll of barbed wire. He resisted the fat lad's attack successfully and the two struggled all over the level place on which the camp had been pitched.

Finally, however, they approached so near to the edge that Rob interfered.

"You'll roll down the slope into the lake in another minute," he said. "Two baths a day would be too much for Tubby. Besides, he'd raise the water and swamp the canoes."

The fat youth, with a pretence of outraged dignity, sought his tepee and engaged himself in cleaning his twentytwo rifle. After a while, though, he emerged from his temporary obscurity, and joined the group about the fire, who were happily discussing plans.

"One good thing is that we have plenty of arms," volunteered Hiram, "in case Hunt and his gang attack us we can easily keep them off."

"Good gracious!" exclaimed the professor, "surely you don't contemplate any such unlawful acts, major?"

"As shooting at folks you mean," laughed the major. "No indeed, my dear professor. But if those rascals attack us I hope we shall be able to tackle them without any other weapons than those nature has given us."

"I owe Freeman Hunt a good punch," muttered Tubby. "I'd like to make the dust fly around his heels with this rifle."

"Goodness, you talk like a regular 'Alkali Ike'," grinned Hiram.

"Bet you I could hit an apple at two hundred yards with this rifle, anyway," asserted the stout youth.

"Bet my hunting knife you can't."

"All right, we'll try tomorrow. This rifle is a dandy, I tell you."

"Pooh! It won't carry a hundred yards."

"It won't, eh? It'll carry half a mile, the man who sold it to me said so."

"Minds me uv er gun my uncle had daown in Virginny," put in Jumbo who had been an interested listener, "that thar gun was ther mos' umbliquitos gun I ever hearn' tell uv."

"It was a long distance shooter, eh?" laughed the major, scenting some fun.

"Long distance, sah! Why, majah, sah, dat gun hadn't no ekil fo' long distancenessness. Dat gun 'ud shootit 'ud shoot de eye out uv er lilly fly des as fur as you could see."

"It would, really, Jumbo?" inquired Andy Bowles, deeply interested.

"It sho' would fer sartain shuh, Massa Bowles."

"Pshaw, that's nothing," scoffed Tubby, with a wink at the others. The funloving youth scented a joke. "My uncle had a gun that once killed a deer at three miles."

"At free miles, Massa Hopkins?"

"Yes. It sounds incredible I know, but they had the state surveyor measure off the ground and sure enough it was three miles."

"Umho!" exclaimed Jumbo, blinking at the fire, "dat's a wun'ful gun shoh 'nuff. But mah uncle's gun hed it beat."

"Impossible, Jumbo!" exclaimed the major.

"Yas, sah, it deed. Mah uncle's gun done cahhey so fah dat mah uncle he done hed ter put salt on his bullets befo' he fahed dem."

"Put salt on his bullets before he fired them, Jumbo! What on earth for?" demanded Rob while the others bent forward interestedly.

"Jes' becos of de distance at which dat rifle killed," explained Jumbo. "Yo' see, and especially in warm weather, dat salt was needed, 'cos it took mah uncle such a time te git to it after he done kill it dat if those bullets weren't salted the game would hev spoiled. Yes, sah, da's a fac', majah."

A dead silence fell over the camp at the conclusion of this interesting narrative. You could have heard a pin drop. At last the major said, in a solemn voice:

"Jumbo, I fear you are an exaggerator."

"Ah specs' ah is, majah. I specs' ah is, but you know dat zaggerators is bo'n and not made, lak potes."

Then the laughter broke loose. The hillside echoed with it, and Jumbo, who deemed that he had been called a most complimentary term by the major, gazed from one to the other in a highly puzzled way.

“Reminds me of old Uncle Hank who keeps a grocery store near my uncle’s farm up in Vermont,” put in Hiram. “One night in the store they were talking about potato bugs. One old fellow said he had seen twenty potato bugs on one stalk.

“‘Pshaw!’ said an old man named Abner Deene, ‘that’s nothing. Why, up in my potato patch they’ve eaten everything up and now when I go outdoors I kin see ’em sitting around the lot, on trees and fences, waitin’ fer me ter plant over ag’in.’

“Then it came the turn of an old fellow named Cyrus Harper. Cyrus laughed at Abner.

“‘Sittin’ roun’ on fences,’ he sniffed, ‘that’s nuffin’. Nuffin’ at all. Why whar I come from the potato bugs come right into the kitchen, open the oven doors and yank the red hot baking potatoes out of the stove.’

“My uncle hadn’t said a thing all this time, but now he struck in.

“‘Gentlemen,’ he said, ‘all these potatobug stories don’t begin to compare with the breed they had down near Brattleboro, where I come from. Down there I used to clerk in Si Toner’s grocery and general store. Well, the potato bugs used to come into the store in the spring and look over Si’s books to see who’d been buying potato seed.’”

“Funny thing your uncle never met the wonderful rifle shot, Philander Potts,” said the professor musingly, after the laughter over Hiram’s yarn had subsided.

“Philander Potts,” exclaimed the boys, “never heard of him.”

“Too bad,” said the professor musingly, “he was the best shot in the world, too, I guess. Why, once he undertook to fire at a rubber target , times in two minutes. The way he did it was this. He had a repeating rifle and kept firing as fast as he could at the indiarubber target. The bullets would bounce off and he caught them in the muzzle of his rifle as they flew back and fired them over again.”

“But what about the bullets that were coming out? Didn’t they collide with the ones coming back?” asked Andy Bowles in all seriousness.

“No,” said the professor gravely, “you see, Philander was so swift in his movements that he was able to fire and catch alternately.”

“I’ll have to practice that,” laughed Tubby.

Soon after the narration of this surprising anecdote, the major looked at his watch.

"Bless my soul!" he exclaimed, "nine o'clock. Time for lights out. Andy, sound 'Taps' and we'll post the sentries for the night."

Tubby and Hiram were selected for the first watch. The major and young Andy were to stand the second vigil while the third period of sentry duty fell to Merritt and Rob. It seemed to the latter that they had not been asleep half an hour when the major entered their tepee and aroused them for their tour of duty. He reported all quiet, and a clear moonlight night.

Hastily throwing on their uniforms the Boy Scouts turned out. For some time they paced their posts steadfastly without anything occurring to mar the stillness of the night. The moon shone down brightly, silvering the surface of the lake which could be glimpsed through the dark trees.

Suddenly Rob, who had reached the limit of his post, which was not far from where the canoes had been hauled up, was startled by a slight sound. It ceased almost instantly, but presently it occurred again.

Cautiously the boy crept through the forest toward the water's edge. He took every advantage of his scout training and carefully avoided treading on twigs or anything that might cause a sound of his approach to be made manifest.

Gliding from tree trunk to tree trunk he soon arrived at the spot in which the canoes had been dragged ashore. At the same instant he became aware of several dark figures moving about among them. Suddenly, right behind him, a twig snapped. In the stillness it sounded as loud as the report of a pistol. Rob wheeled round swiftly, but not before a figure leaped toward him from behind a tree trunk. Before Rob could raise a hand in selfdefense another form sprang at him.

The lad tried to cry out and discharge his rifle, but before he could accomplish either act he was felled by some heavy instrument, and a gag thrust into his mouth. The next instant, bound and incapable of uttering a sound, he was borne swiftly toward the canoes.

CHAPTER XII.

CAPTURED.

But silently as the attack upon Rob had been made, it had not taken place without causing some disturbance. Moreover, the sharp crack of the snapping twig which had attracted Rob's attention to his trailers, had also reached Merritt's sharp ears. In the silence of the nightenwrapped forest sounds carry far.

Merritt was all attention in a flash. The snap of the twig might have been caused by some prying animal or

"Gee whiz! That's the scuffling of feet!" exclaimed the young sentry the next moment as the sounds of the tussle came to him.

His first act was to fire a shot. It should have been aimed in the air, but in his excitement Merritt fired low. The bullet whizzed in the direction of the camp, struck a tin kettle which was piled up with a number of other tin utensils, and brought the whole pile down with a crash. Now Jumbo's chosen sleeping place was right behind this barricade of tin hardware. When it fell it came crashing about the colored man in an earsplitting avalanche. Jumbo leaped to his feet with a howl. He was attired in his shirt, trousers and shoes, not having bothered to remove these when he retired.

"Fo' de lan's sake what dat gum gophulous racket?" he yelled. In a flash his long legs began to move.

"Ah'll bet a pint uv peanuts dat's Injuns!" he shouted as he sped along, "mah goodness, ah wish ah had mah uncle's gun. But as ah ain't ah's jes' a gwine te trus' ter mah laigs."

Jumbo, in great leaps and strides, arrived at the lakeside in a few instants. In the meantime, the camp behind him was in an uproar of excitement over the midnight alarm.

The negro had already reached the waterside before he felt himself knocked flat by a heavy blow on the head. Now Jumbo's head, like all negroes', was about as hard as a bit of adamant. But the cowardly fellow deemed it better to lie perfectly still when he was knocked flat. Presently he felt himself being picked up and thrown into something that the next instant began to move off. He realized in a flash that he was lying in the bottom of one of the canoes.

"Hailp! Hailp!" he began to yell, but was silent instantly as a harsh voice breathed in his ear:

"You shut up if you don't want a bullet in your black head."

Jumbo lay silent after that. But his thoughts were busy.

"Bullet in mah haid, eh?" he mused, "mah goodness, ah don't want nuffin' lak dat. Mah cocoanut feels now laik ah'd done tried ter butt a locusmocus off'n de track. Wondah what deportentiousness uv all dis unusualauness done mean?"

His meditations were interrupted by a shout from the shore.

"Bring back those canoes at once!"

"Mah goodness, dat am de majah," exclaimed Jumbo, but to himself. "He shuh am po'ful mad. Wondah if dem boys is playin' pranks. If dey is dey'll be sorry fer it."

The black ventured to raise his head a little and peep up to see who was in the canoe with him. In doing so his eyes fell on another figure lying beside him. In the moonlight he could see the cords that bound it. The radiance of the moon also revealed the Boy Scout uniform.

"Gabriel's Ho'hn! Dat's one of dem Boy Scrouts!" he exclaimed, "an' mah gracious, ah wondah who dat fierce lookin' man am whose paddlin' dis yar boat. Reckon ah'd better lay quiet. He looks pretty frambunctious."

In the meantime, the aroused inmates of the camp had rushed to the shore. They reached it just in time to see their entire flotilla of canoes being paddled swiftly off across the smooth, moonlit waters. Tubby and Hiram raised their rifles when a hoarse laugh of defiance greeted the major's command to the marauders to halt. But in a flash the officer saw what they were about to do.

"None of that, boys," he ordered sharply, "put down those rifles."

"No use for them now," grumbled Tubby, "see, they've disappeared round that point."

"Let's get after them," suggested Hiram.

The major shook his head.

“Over this rough ground they could easily outdistance us,” he said, “is anyone missing?”

It took but a few minutes to ascertain that both Rob and Jumbo were not among them.

“This is even more serious than the theft of the canoes,” exclaimed the professor, “do you suppose that it was Hunt’s gang that took them?”

“I don’t doubt it,” said the major, “who else would be interested in annoying us? But let’s hear Merritt’s story. What did you hear, my boy?”

Merritt soon told his narrative of the crackling twig and the struggle. A visit to the beach showed that there had, indeed, been a struggle before Rob had been landed in the canoe. A disconsolate silence fell on the little party.

“What are we to do now?” wondered Hiram.

“Get in pursuit of them as quick as possible, I should think,” opined Tubby.

The major shook his head.

“Not much use in that,” he decided, “we would not be likely to find them. No, the best plan is to wait right here. If Rob escapes he will be able to find his way back again.”

“Do you think they mean him harm?” inquired little Andy Bowles tremulously.

“I hardly think so,” responded the major, “they wouldn’t dare to do much more than keep him prisoner. But even that’s bad enough.”

“But what object can they have in all this except to annoy us?” asked the professor.

“Simple enough,” said the major, rather bitterly, “I guess they are going to hold Rob as a hostage.”

“What do you mean?”

“That if they manage to keep him prisoner we shan’t see him again till I have given them the plans to the location of the Dangerfield treasure cave.”

“They wouldn’t dare” began the professor. But the major interrupted him.

“We have already had a proof of what they will dare,” he said, “they are as desperate a band of ruffians as I have ever heard of.”

“I guess that’s right,” agreed Tubby, “but I’ll bet,” he added stoutly, “that Rob will find a way out of it yet.”

In the meantime the canoes sped on through the night. Rob mentally tried to keep some track of the distance traversed, but he was totally unable to do so. He judged, however, when the paddles finally ceased their splashing, that they must have come some distance, for it was daybreak when the canoes came to a halt.

Rob was roughly jerked to his feet and then, for the first time, became aware of Jumbo. For his back had been toward the negro in the canoe.

“Mah goodness, Marse Blake,” exclaimed the black, “ain’ dis de mostes’ parallelxillus sintuation dat you ever seen. Ah declar’”

But further remarks on Jumbo’s part were roughly checked by the man who had paddled the two prisoners to their present situation. He was none other than the biglimbed rascal, Jim Dale, who had played such a prominent part in the theft of the pocketbook.

“Shut your black head, nigger,” he ordered gruffly.

“Ah ain’t no niggah. Ah’s a ’spectabilious colored gent”; protested Jumbo, “’nd I kain’t shut mah haid nohow ’cos it keeps openin’ an’ shuttin’ of its own accord whar you busted me on it.”

But a fierce look from the man made even the garrulous negro subside. As for Rob, he disdained to talk to the fellow, or bandy words with him. Instead, he gazed around while the other canoes, filched from the Boy Scout camp, were coming up. He noted that one was paddled by Peter Bumpus, while the third one contained Stonington Hunt and his son Freeman, the lad who had already given the Boy Scouts so much trouble.

It was a curious place in which the boy found himself. But Rob, with his scout instinct, could not but admire the skill with which it had been chosen as a retreat.

The spot was like a large basin with steep rock walls on all sides but one. On the open side a narrow neck of the lake led into this natural fortress. Great trees and luxurious water growth masked the entrance and anybody, not knowing of it, might have passed by it on the lake side a hundred times without noting its presence. The canoes had been paddled through this natural screen of water maples and rank growth of all kinds, which had closed like a curtain behind them.

A beach, narrow except at the far end of the cove, ran round the water's edge at the foot of the rocky walls. A small tent was pitched there, and a fire was smoldering. Evidently the place had been occupied for some little time as a camp. Rob found himself wondering how the men, in whose power he now was, had ever found the place. He did not know then that Jim Dale and Pete Bumpus had once been associated with a gang of moonshiners, whose retreat this had been before the officers of the revenue service broke the gang up and scattered them far and wide.

Hunt had gleaned enough knowledge from the plan, during his brief possession of it, to divine which route the party would take to the hidden treasure trove. He had, therefore, sought out this place when Dale and Bumpus told him of it. The boys' enemies had made straight for it, and had been encamped there some days awaiting the arrival of the party. The notes of Andy Bowles' bugle floating out across the lake the night before had apprised them of the arrival of the party, and plans had immediately been made for a hasty descent on the Boy Scouts' mountain camp. How successful it had proved we already know. But of course, to Rob, all this was a mystery.

The canoes were grounded at the end of the cove on the broad strip of beach. Rob and Jumbo were at once ordered to get out, and Rob's legbonds being loosened and gag removed, he followed Jumbo on to the white sand. Hardly had their feet touched it before Stonington Hunt and his rascally young son, the latter with a sneer on his face, also landed.

"Fell neatly into our little trap, didn't you?" jeered Stonington Hunt, staring straight at Rob with an insolent look.

"Yo' alls kin hev yo' trap fo' all I wants uv it"; snorted Jumbo indignantly, as Rob disdained to answer.

“Be quiet, you black idiot!” snapped Hunt, “we didn’t want you, anyhow. I’ve a good mind,” he went on with a brutal sort of humor, “to have you thrown into the lake.”

“By golly yo’ jes bring on de man to do it,” exclaimed the negro with great bravado, “ah reckon ah kin tackle him. Ah’m frum Vahgeenyah, ah is, an”

But Hunt impatiently checked him. He turned to Peter Bumpus. “Cook us up a meal,” he ordered.

“For them, too?” asked Bumpus, jerking his thumb backward at Rob and Jumbo.

“Of course. You may as well get used to it. I expect they’ll make quite a long stay with us.”

Rob’s heart sank. He was a lad who always schooled himself to look on the brightest side of things. But no gleam of hope lightened the gloom of their present situation. Things could not have been much worse, he felt.

CHAPTER XIII.

ROB FINDS A RAY OF HOPE.

The meal, a sort of stew composed apparently of rabbits, partridges and other small game, was despatched and then Rob, who had been released from his bonds while he ate, was tied up once more.

"These fellows don't think much of breaking the game laws," he thought as he ruminated on the contents of the big iron pot from which their noonday meal had been served. Then came another thought. If they so openly violated the laws, the country was surely a lonely one, and seldom, or never, visited. Indeed, the thick forest of hemlock and other coniferous trees that fringed the cliff summits, would seem to indicate that the spot was well chosen.

Jumbo was not confined. The gang seemed to esteem him as more or less harmless for, although a sharp watch was kept on him, he was not fettered. Once or twice he caught Rob's eye with a knowing look. But he said nothing. One or another of the men kept too close and constant a watch for that. And so the hours wore on. Tied as Rob was, the small black flies and other winged mountain pests made life almost intolerable. With infinite pains the lad dragged himself to a spot of shade under a stunted alder bush. He lay here with something very like despair clutching coldly at his heart. The canoes had been anchored, with big stones attached to ropes, at some distance out in the little bay. Only one remained on shore, and by that Jim Dale kept an unrelaxing vigil.

Jim and Peter were talking in low voices. Rob overheard enough to know that their talk was of the old lawless days when the moonshine gang made the hidden cove their rendezvous.

"Those were the days," Dale said with a regretful sigh, "money was plenty then. By the way, Pete, did you ever hear what became of Black Bart and the others after the revenues broke us up?"

"No, I never wanted to take a chance of inquiring," rejoined Peter, puffing at a dirty corn cob. "I did hear, though, that they had resumed operations some place around here."

"They did, eh? I suppose they figgered that lightning don't never strike twice in the same place."

"Just the same, they are taking a long chance. With revenues against you it's all one sidedlike the handle of a jug."

"That's so. But there's good money in it, and Black Bart would risk a lot for that."

The conversation was carried on in low tones. Rob, intent though he was, could not catch any more of it. But he pondered over what he had heard. If what Jim Dale and Peter had said was correct, a gang of moonshiners still made the mountains thereabouts their habitat.

"It's a strange situation we've stumbled into," thought the boy.

Then he fell to observing Stonington Hunt and his son, Freeman. The man and the boy were talking earnestly at some distance from Peter and Jim Dale. From their gestures and expressions Rob made out that the conversation was an important one. From the frequent glances which they cast in his direction he also divined that he himself, was, in all probability, the subject of it.

All at once Stonington Hunt arose and came toward him. Freeman followed him. They came straight up to Rob and stood over him.

"Well, Rob Blake," sneered young Hunt, "I guess things are different to what they were the time you drove me out of Hampton and forced my father to profess all sorts of reformation."

"I don't know," rejoined Rob coolly and contemptuously, "you seem to me to be very much the same sort of a chap you were then."

The inference, and Rob's unshaken manner, appeared to infuriate the youth.

"We've got you where we want you now," he snarled, "it would serve you right if I took all the trouble you've caused us out upon your hide. You and that patrol of yours cost us our social position, then that Hopkins kid lost our sloop for us"

"The sloop in which you meant to decamp with the major's papers," put in Rob in the same calm tones, "don't try to assume any better position than that of a common thief, Freeman."

With a quick snarl of rage the boy jumped on the helpless and bound boy. He brought his fist down on Rob's face with all his force. Then he fastened his hands in Rob's hair and tugged with all his might. But suddenly something happened. Something that startled young Hunt considerably.

Rob gave a quick twist and despite his bonds managed to half raise himself. In this position he gave the other lad such a terrific "butt" that Freeman was sent staggering backward, with a white face. Unable to regain his balance he presently fell flat on the sand. He scrambled to his feet and seized a big bit of timber, the limb of a hemlock that lay close at hand. He was advancing, brandishing this with the intention of annihilating Rob when Stonington Hunt, who had hitherto been an impassive observer, stepped between them.

"Here, here, what's all this?" he snapped angrily. "This isn't a fighting ring. Put down that stick, Freeman, and you, young Blake, listen to me."

"I'm listening," said Rob, in the same cold, impassive way that had so irritated Freeman.

"You want to regain your freedom and rejoin your friends, don't you?" was the next question.

"If it can be done by honorable meansyes. But I doubt if you can employ such, after what I've seen of you."

"Hard words won't mend matters," rejoined Hunt with a frown, "after all, I've as much right to this hidden treasure as anyone elseif I can get it."

"Yes, if you can get it," replied Rob with meaning emphasis, wondering much what could be coming next.

"Your liberty depends on my getting it," resumed Hunt.

"My liberty?" echoed the boy, "how is that?"

"I want you to write a note to Major Dangerfield. He thinks a good deal of you, doesn't he?"

"I hope so," responded Rob, mightily curious to know what Hunt was driving at.

“He’s responsible, too, in a way, for your safety, isn’t he? I mean your parents rely on him to bring you back safe and sound?”

“I suppose so. But why don’t you come to the point. Tell me what it is you want.”

“Just this: You write to the major. I’ll see that the note is delivered. You must tell him to give my messenger the plan and map of the treasure’s hiding place. If he does so you will be returned safe and sound. So will the nigger and the canoes. We didn’t want that nigger anyhow. In the darkness we mistook him for the major.”

Rob could hardly repress a smile at the idea of the dignified major being confused with the ubiquitous Jumbo.

“Are you willing to write such a letter?”

“You mean am I willing to stake my safety against the major’s hopes of recovering his relative’s hidden fortune?”

“That’s about ityes.”

Rob’s mind worked quickly. It might be dangerous to give a direct negative and yet he certainly would have refused to do as the rascal opposite to him suggested.

“IICan you give me time to think it over?” he hesitated, assuming uncertainty in decision.

“Yes, I’ll give you a reasonable period. But mind, no shillyshallying. Don’t entertain any idea of escape. You’ll be guarded as closely here as if you were in a stonewalled prison.”

“I know that,” said Rob, feeling an inward conviction that Hunt’s words were literally true. The cliffenclosed cove was indeed a prison. Hunt turned away, followed by his son. The latter cast a malevolent look back at Rob as he went.

“My! His father must be proud of that lad,” thought Rob.

Hunt and his followers fell to playing cards. Rob was left to his reflections. Jumbo sat gloomily apart and yet in full view of the card players. After a while Rob’s thoughts reverted to the conversation he had overheard between Dale and Peter Bumpus. In this connection he suddenly bethought himself of something. Jim Dale had spoken of the revenue officers raiding the moonshiners' plant. If that was the case, and the miscreants had all escaped, how did they go?

The revenue officers probably attacked the place from the lake side of the cove. This would have effectually shut off all hope of escape in that direction. The only conclusion left, to account for the freedom of the gang was a startling one.

The cove must have some secret entrance or exit. If such were the case it could only be by a passage or by steps cut in the seemingly solid rock. Rob's heart began to beat a bit faster. There might be a chance of escape after all, if only he could discover the means of exit he was now certain must exist somewhere in the cove.

But a careful scrutiny failed to show any indications of such a device as he was looking for. The walls were bare and clean as cliffs of marble. Not more than two or three stunted conifers grew out of an occasional crevice. The enclosing walls would not have afforded footing to a fly.

"Guess I was wrong," thought Rob to himself and lying back on the sand he closed his eyes the better to concentrate his thoughts. But what with the strain of the early hours and the warm, sultry atmosphere, the lad found his ideas wandering. Presently, without knowing it, he had dropped off into a sound slumber.

When he awoke it was with a start. The long shadows showed him that the day was far spent. All at once voices near at hand struck in upon his half awakened senses.

Rob heard a few words and then, with wildly beating pulses, he fell to simulating sleep with all his might. From what he had heard of the conversation he believed that a hope of escape lay in the words of the talkers.